PRACTICE MAKES PERFECT

What Reviewers Say About Carsen Taite's Work

Pursuit of Happiness

"This was a quick, fun and sexy read. …It was enjoyable to read about a political landscape filled with out-and-proud LGBTQIA+ folks winning elections."—Katie Pierce, Librarian

"An out presidential candidate (Meredith Mitchell) who is not afraid to follow her heart during campaigning. That is truly utopia. A public defender (Stevie Palmer) who is leery about getting involved with the would-be president. The two women are very interesting characters. The author does an excellent job of keeping their jobs in focus while creating a wonderful romance around the campaign and intense media focus. …Taite has written a book that draws you in. It had us hooked from the first paragraph to the last."—*Best Lesfic Reviews*

Love's Verdict

"Carsen Taite excels at writing legal thrillers with lesbian main characters using her experience as a criminal defense attorney."
—*Lez Review Books*

Outside the Law

"[A] fabulous closing to the Lone Star Law Series. …Tanner and Sydney's journey back to each other is sweet, sexy and sure to keep you entertained."—*The Romantic Reader Blog*

"This is by far the best book of the series and Ms. Taite has saved the best for last. Each book features a romance and the main characters, Tanner Cohen and Sydney Braswell are well rounded, lovable and their chemistry is sizzling. …The book found the perfect balance between romance and thriller with a surprising twist at the end. Very entertaining read. Overall, a very good end of this series. Recommended for both romance and thriller fans. 4.5 stars."
—*Lez Review Books*

A More Perfect Union

"[*A More Perfect Union*] is a fabulously written tightly woven political/military intrigue with a large helping of romance. I enjoyed every minute and was on the edge of my seat the whole time. This one is a great read! Carsen Taite never disappoints!"
—*The Romantic Reader Blog*

"Readers looking for a mix of intrigue and romance set against a political backdrop will want to pick up Taite's latest novel."
—*Romantic Times Book Review*

Sidebar

"As always a well written novel from Carsen Taite. The two main characters are well developed, likeable, and have sizzling chemistry."—Melina Bickard, Librarian, Waterloo Library (UK)

"Sidebar is a love story with a refreshing twist. It's a mystery and a bit of a thriller, with an ethical dilemma and some subterfuge thrown in for good measure. The combination gives us a fast-paced read, which includes courtroom and personal drama, an appealing love story, and a more than satisfying ending."—*Lambda Literary Review*

Letter of the Law

"If you like romantic suspense novels, stories that involve the law, or anything to do with ranching, you're not going to want to miss this one."—*The Lesbian Review*

Without Justice

"This is a great read, fast paced, interesting and takes a slightly different tack from the normal crime/courtroom drama. ...I really enjoyed immersing myself in this rapid fire adventure. Suspend your disbelief, take the plunge, it's definitely worth the effort."
—*Lesbian Reading Room*

"Carsen Taite tells a great story. She is consistent in giving her readers a good if not great legal drama with characters who are insightful, well thought out and have good chemistry. You know when you pick up one of her books you are getting your money's worth time and time again. Consistency with a great legal drama is all but guaranteed."—*The Romantic Reader Blog*

Above the Law

"...readers who enjoyed the first installment will find this a worthy second act."—*Publishers Weekly*

Reasonable Doubt

"I liked everything. The story is perfectly paced and plotted, and the characters had me rooting for them. It has a damn good first kiss too."—*The Lesbian Review*

Lay Down the Law

"This book is AMAZING!!! The setting, the scenery, the people, the plot, wow. ...I loved Peyton's tough-on-the-outside, crime fighting, intensely protective of those who are hers, badass self."
—*Prism Book Alliance*

"I've enjoyed all of Carsen Taite's previous novels and this one was no different. The main characters were well-developed and intriguing, the supporting characters came across as very 'real' and the storyline was really gripping. The twists and turns had me so hooked I finished the book in one sitting."—Melina Bickard, Librarian, Waterloo Library (London)

Courtship

"Taite (*Switchblade*) keeps the stakes high as two beautiful and brilliant women fueled by professional ambitions face daunting emotional choices. ...As backroom politics, secrets, betrayals, and threats race to be resolved without political damage to the president, the cat-and-mouse relationship game between Addison and Julia has the reader rooting for them. Taite prolongs the fever-pitch tension to the final pages. This pleasant read with intelligent heroines, snappy dialogue, and political suspense will satisfy Taite's devoted fans and new readers alike."—*Publishers Weekly*

Switchblade

"I enjoyed the book and it was a fun read—mystery, action, humour, and a bit of romance. Who could ask for more? If you've read and enjoyed Taite's legal novels, you'll like this. If you've read and enjoyed the two other books in this series, this one will definitely satisfy your Luca fix and I highly recommend picking it up. Highly recommended."—*C-Spot Reviews*

Battle Axe

"This second book is satisfying, substantial, and slick. Plus, it has heart and love coupled with Luca's array of weapons and a bad-ass verbal repertoire. ...I cannot imagine anyone not having a great time riding shotgun through all of Luca's escapades. I recommend hopping on Luca's band wagon and having a blast."—*Rainbow Book Reviews*

Beyond Innocence

"As you would expect, sparks and legal writs fly. What I liked about this book were the shades of grey (no, not the smutty Shades of Grey)—both in the relationship as well as the cases."—*C-spot Reviews*

Nothing but the Truth

"Taite has written an excellent courtroom drama with two interesting women leading the cast of characters. Taite herself is a practicing defense attorney, and her courtroom scenes are clearly based on real knowledge. This should be another winner for Taite."—*Lambda Literary*

It Should be a Crime—Lammy Finalist

"Taite breathes life into her characters with elemental finesse. ...A great read, told in the vein of a good old detective-type novel filled with criminal elements, thugs, and mobsters that will entertain and amuse."—*Lambda Literary*

Visit us at www.boldstrokesbooks.com

By the Author

Truelesbianlove.com
It Should be a Crime
Do Not Disturb
Nothing but the Truth
The Best Defense
Beyond Innocence
Rush
Courtship
Reasonable Doubt
Without Justice
Sidebar
A More Perfect Union
Love's Verdict
Pursuit of Happiness

The Luca Bennett Mystery Series:
Slingshot
Battle Axe
Switchblade
Bow and Arrow (novella in Girls with Guns)

Lone Star Law Series:
Lay Down the Law
Above the Law
Letter of the Law
Outside the Law

Legal Affairs Romances:
Practice Makes Perfect

Practice Makes Perfect

by

Carsen Taite

2019

PRACTICE MAKES PERFECT

ISBN 13: 978-1-63555-357-4

This Trade Paperback Original Is Published By
Bold Strokes Books, Inc.
P.O. Box 249
Valley Falls, NY 12185

First Edition: June 2019

CREDITS
Editor: Cindy Cresap
Production Design: Susan Ramundo
Cover Design By Jeanine Henning

Acknowledgments

As much as I enjoy a dark mystery or a gripping crime drama, I'm a sucker for pure romance where the biggest element of suspense is will they or won't they get together even when I know there's going to be a happily ever after. If the story makes me laugh and cry during the journey, it's a total bonus. The Legal Affairs series, beginning with this book, is a bit of a departure from many of my previous books. It's lighter fare, but you'll still find strong women and, of course there will be lawyers. I like to call it love and law, but without any lawlessness. I hope you enjoy!

Thanks always to Rad and Sandy for making the best publishing house on the planet feel like a home. Thanks to Jeanine Henning for a cohesive and hot set of covers for this series. To my intrepid editor Cindy Cresap—thanks for pushing me to be better with each book with your smart insights and hilarious sense of humor.

Thanks to Georgia Beers for our daily check-ins. There were some days I'd rather do just about anything than rack up a word count, but knowing we were in it together kept me on track.

Ruth and Paula, thanks for being my literary lawyer pals, always available to strategize. And, Paula, special thanks to you for reading drafts of this story right up until the moment I turned it in. Your insight and feedback was invaluable—you're the best!

Jane Chen and Nell Stark—thanks for the fruitful brainstorming session about Leaderboard. Love bouncing ideas around with you.

Dreams are so much more attainable when you have someone to encourage you along the way. Thanks to my wife, Lainey, for always believing in my dreams even when they involve sacrificing our time together. I couldn't do this without you.

And to my loyal readership, thank you, thank you, thank you. Every time you purchase one of my stories, you give me the gift of allowing me to make a living doing what I love. Thanks for taking this journey with me.

Dedication

To Lainey. There's no one I'd rather dream with than you.

CHAPTER ONE

All ideas were good ideas after two shots of tequila. The thought skimmed the surface of Campbell Clark's mind as she rolled the full shot glass between her fingers. She was seated at a table, tucked away in the corner of Azul, the rooftop bar of the Westin in downtown Austin, with her two best friends from law school, Abby Keane and Grace Maldonado. Seemingly a safe, private place to reveal the grand plan that had just popped into her head, but until today's five-year law school reunion, she hadn't seen Grace and Abby in over a year, and she wasn't sure if they would fist-bump her idea or tell the waitress to cut her off.

Rewind to earlier in the day when she'd been standing in her closet trying to decide if the dressy casual dress code was more dressy or casual, and wanting to throttle whoever had come up with the term. For tonight's reunion mixer, she'd settled on dark blue, slim fit jeans, a royal blue top, her favorite cognac moto jacket, and the brand new pair of peep toe booties she'd splurged on at Neiman's last week, using the excuse that a class reunion was the perfect reason to buy something new. Plus she was celebrating seeing Grace and Abby for the first time in way too long. During their three years in law school, they'd been inseparable, but after graduation, they'd scattered to separate cities—Grace in Houston, Abby in Dallas, while Campbell stayed in Austin—each of them lured by the prospect of big firms, big paychecks, big opportunities. They'd sworn they would stay in touch.

And they had. Kind of. They talked at least once a quarter and Skyped when they could, more often than not each of them sitting at their desks with piles of files in the background, but the actually getting together part had consisted of exactly two occasions in the past five years, both of which were at annual meetings of the state bar where they'd shared stories about their jobs but hadn't discussed anything personal because who had time for a personal life when you were trying to make partner?

When she'd arrived at the hotel an hour earlier, Campbell had scoured the ballroom packed with several hundred UT law school alumni, but neither Grace nor Abby were in sight, and she made her way to the bar to grab a drink while she waited for them to arrive. She stopped along the way to catch up with several of her acquaintances from school, all the while scanning the room to keep an eye out for her friends. After almost an hour, she finally made it to the crowd at the bar, but before she could join the long line, she was distracted by a bellowing voice, yelling her name.

"Campbell!"

She turned at the sound of her name, and hid a frown when she saw who it was. Ronald Burch had graduated number one in their class and was walking, talking proof that book smarts only had limited value. "Hi, Ron," she said, using the shortened version of his name because she knew it drove him crazy. "What's shakin'?"

"I'm sure you've heard I am on the short list for a Supreme Court clerkship for the upcoming term."

"That's great news." Campbell resisted asking him what had taken so long, but silently prayed that whichever justice interviewed him for the position would see past his sharp legal mind and realize Ron possessed very little ability to connect with actual humans, a skill she deemed necessary for anyone who either was a judge or worked for them.

"It is great news, indeed," Ron said, giving no indication he detected her enthusiasm for his news was feigned. "I'm already looking at apartments in DC. Affordable housing is difficult to come by."

"I'm sure you'll find something, and if you're hired, they'll probably be able to connect you with some resources."

Ron leaned toward her, so closely invading her space that she could smell the garlic from the bruschetta he'd stuffed in his mouth right after he'd called out to her. "I don't think there's any *if* about it. My sources tell me I'm exactly the type of scholar Justice Cohen is looking for."

His upraised eyebrows signaled he was waiting for her to agree, but even though she didn't want to be mean to him, she wouldn't inflate his super ego. Thankfully, at that moment, she heard someone calling her name again, and this time she was certain it was someone she wanted to talk to. Make that two someones. "Grace, Abby!" she yelled to her friends who were walking toward her. She stepped toward them and whispered, "I can't even tell you how happy I am to see you."

"Are you sure?" Abby said, wearing a playful smile. "Because if you're busy, we can catch up with you later."

"Stop it," Campbell said, pulling both Abby and Grace into a hug. She leaned back to drink in the sight of them and, keeping her voice low, she said."Can we find another bar in this hotel, because I've been trying to get to this one for the last hour and that's too long to settle for whatever house brands they're pouring."

"Deal," said Grace. "Lead the way."

Campbell told Ron they had a super important privileged legal matter to discuss, hooked a friend on each arm, and led them out of the ballroom to the elevators. On the way up to the rooftop bar, she gave them a hard time about being late. "Especially you, Grace. I've never known you to show up late for anything."

"I tried to leave in time to avoid crazy traffic, but one of the partners caught me heading out and fobbed off research he needs for a motion due on Monday. I'll probably have to head back tonight to get it done on time."

"What about the dinner tomorrow night?" Campbell asked.

Grace shook her head. "Not in the cards."

"I may have to miss too," Abby said. "We've got jury selection starting on Monday. I was barely able to make it at all."

The elevator dinged, and they walked out into the rooftop bar and snagged a table overlooking the city of Austin. In direct contrast to the long line downstairs, a server approached them within seconds and they ordered drinks. Campbell smiled when she saw nothing about that had changed. Tequila for her, an extra dirty martini for Abby, and Grace ordered a Manhattan. They spent a few minutes dishing about the rest of their class, but when the waiter arrived with their cocktails, Campbell raised her glass and toasted their success. "Okay, so spill," she said. "What've you all been up to?" She reached for the bar snacks and started munching while she waited for them to respond.

"I've been working on a class action pharmaceutical case," Abby said. "It's a nightmare because the witnesses are all over the country. I haven't slept in my own bed more than one night a week for the last six months."

Campbell nudged her shoulder. "Let me guess, you've got a girl on call in every city." She was surprised by Abby's scowl. "What?"

"As if I had the time or energy for sex. The senior partner of our division always insists on traveling with us, and his motto is if you're not traveling on the client's dime, then you will work every freaking minute of the day. Besides, he likes to put on a show of being frugal, and I'm not about to bring some one-night stand back to whatever version of Motel 6 exists in anywhere USA."

Grace jumped in. "Ouch. I hear you. I'm not traveling, but we've got this crazy product liability case and it's an all hands on deck affair. I'm thinking about ordering a sleeper sofa for my office."

Campbell sipped her Casamigos, and shook her head. Their talk of pending cases had her mind spinning about the six deposition transcripts piled on her desk that needed to be reviewed by Monday, and her angst level was on the rise. "Let's talk about something besides work. I want to hear what else has been going on. Fun, family, love. Grace, you start. Spill."

Grace took a big swallow of her drink, set the thick glass on the table, and folded her hands like she was about to give a presentation. "Well, I saw *Hamilton* on Broadway last month." She grinned. "Box seats, and Lin Manuel-Miranda was on hand for the show."

Campbell nodded with approval. Grace was a total history buff, and *Hamilton* was a perfect fit for her, but she wanted to know more. "Now that's what I'm talking about. How long were you in the city? Where did you stay? Where did you eat? Out with it."

"I was there a week, but most of it was for client meetings. The hotel restaurant was pretty good."

"Seriously?"

Grace shrugged. "I'll go back again and do the town after I've made partner, but this time was strictly a work trip. Hell, I snuck out of the evening prep sessions to make it to the show. I don't think it hurt me to miss, but you never know…"

Her voice trailed off into a sad little sigh, and Campbell felt her own angst level rising again. She turned to Abby. "Your turn. Name at least two fun things you've done since I've seen you last."

Abby munched on an olive. "Two huh? Well, I bought a new car. A BMW M5. She's beautiful and fast as blazes. Although she doesn't get a lot of action since I live so close to the office I usually walk to work. One day I'm going to take her on a road trip. Top down, pushing one twenty, daring some hot woman in a uniform to chase me down."

Campbell snapped her fingers to shake Abby out of her dreams. "I'm not sure buying a car qualifies as a fun thing. What's the other thing?"

"Other thing what?"

"Try to keep up. Fun thing since I last saw you—go!"

"Hmm, let me think." Abby fiddled with the toothpick. She speared another olive and chewed on it with a thoughtful expression while Campbell tapped her fingers on the table. "Yeah, I'm going to have to get back to you on that."

Campbell folded her arms. "Are you telling me that neither one of you can come up with a legit example of the fruits of your success?"

"Now wait a minute," Grace said. "I've got plenty of fruit. It just happens to be in a high-yield investment account with my broker."

"Every girl's dream." Campbell rolled her eyes.

"What am I supposed to do? I don't have time to go on vacation. The only clothes I ever wear are business suits. I barely spend any time at home so there's no point in buying a house." Grace held up her Manhattan. "I buy bourbon by the case. Really good bourbon. From distilleries I plan to visit someday when I have a life. That's something, right?"

"Can you hear yourself? That's pathetic."

"Oh really," Abby chimed in. "I bet you're raking it in on your fifth-year associate salary. Campbell, what do you do with your big bucks?"

Campbell was saved from answering when the waiter showed up with their second round of drinks. He set their glasses on the table and Grace raised hers. "A toast to three soon-to-be law partners. One more year of blood, sweat, and tears, and we'll come into our own."

Campbell clinked her shot glass to Abby's and Grace's drinks, barely suppressing a sigh, but before she could take a drink, Abby reached for her hand.

"What?"

"Before we toast to success, tell us about yours. What have you done for fun lately?"

Campbell hesitated while she cast about for something to say. Shopping at Neiman's wasn't the kind of answer Abby was looking for, but admitting the truth made her feel empty inside, like she'd worked really hard and for what? But the thing that had kept them all friends through the years was the ability to be completely honest with each other, so she took the plunge.

"Nothing." She stared at them and their expectant expressions. Before she could change her mind, she shot nearly the entire glass of expensive extra añejo and clunked her glass back on the table. "I have to confess that my life is about as lame as the two of yours. I spent an hour in my closet this morning looking for something to wear that wasn't a black or navy suit with stylish, but sensible heels. I used to love to shop for clothes, but," she stretched out her leg, "these shoes are the first fun, new thing I've bought in almost a year. When did my life become so boring?"

"When you stopped having one, like the rest of us." Abby fished an olive out of her glass. "I remember the day I got the offer letter from this firm. The very first thing I did was make a list of all the things I was going to do with my newfound wealth." She sighed. "It's on my refrigerator, you know that big box in my kitchen that's empty because I never have time to shop or cook, and I'm never home for meals anyway. And it's not like I have time to meet anyone to cook for."

"Exactly!" Grace slapped her hand on the table. "I've managed to pad my investment accounts and purchase tons of equity in sweet real estate ventures, but for what? If I make it to retirement, I'm going to be an old maid. Nobody wants to be with an old maid. I'll get a cat for company and feed them the finest cat food. Maybe one day someone will find us, cuddled up together, having shared a can of the good stuff, drifting off to a better life where billable hours aren't the be-all end-all of our existence." She sighed and took another drink of her Manhattan.

And that's when the big idea burst into Campbell's brain. She looked down at the last sip in her glass, and then glanced around, contemplating ordering another round of drinks to warm Abby and Grace up to what she was about to say, but the waiter was working a big table across the room, and she knew if she didn't blurt it out soon, she'd lose her nerve. She started to raise her glass, but Abby beat her to it.

"For real this time," Abby said, "We are not, I repeat not, waiting another year before getting together. Get out your calendars. We're making a plan right now."

Grace tipped her glass into the mix. "Deal. And nothing, including demanding partners or billable hours, will get in our way."

Campbell clutched her own shot glass, taking their words as a sign. This was it. Time to say the big idea out loud. She clinked her glass against theirs and tossed back the last swallow of tequila. "I have a plan." She waited a dramatic second until Abby's and Grace's eyes were locked on hers. "Let's start our own firm."

Chapter Two

Later that evening, Campbell hugged Grace and Abby good-bye, and then ducked into the restroom at the hotel one last time before making the trek home. The ladies' room was one of those posh digs with a fancy sitting room, and she paused for a second to look in the mirror to assess her post tequila appearance. Her eyes looked tired, but it was late, so that was to be expected, but she noticed a glimmer in her expression that had been missing for a while, and she chalked it up to the big idea. It had to be. While the idea of starting a new firm was a bit daunting, Grace's and Abby's buy-in, even if tentative, lifted a weight off her shoulders, a weight she hadn't even realized she'd been carrying. The biggest revelation this evening was discovering their lives were as miserable as her own. She'd never stopped to think that the outward trappings of success only covered up a gaping hole of suckage for all of them.

Her mind started racing with more ideas. They would need to rent office space, hire staff, and come up with a marketing campaign. They'd need a website, a logo, branding. That was Abby's thing. Business plans and all that were Grace's strength. Her strength was networking, and they'd agreed that she'd be the firm ambassador of sorts, making the rounds in the business and legal community to drum up new business.

But even divvying up the duties there was a ton to do, and timing was everything. The flood of ideas buffeted her mind back and forth, and Campbell felt dizzy with all the to-dos now on her list. The tequila probably hadn't helped. Some people drunk dialed when they'd had too much to drink, but apparently, she drunk opened a new law firm. The realization that starting a new firm with Grace and Abby meant she was quitting her job with her current firm did nothing to help her fuzzy state, and she decided it was time to get home. She turned away from the mirror, intent on striding outside to get some fresh air and a cab home, but instead, her heel caught on the fancy rug, and she pitched headlong into the arms of a stranger.

Campbell struggled to right herself, but the tall stranger in the form-fitting little black cocktail dress held on. Except she wasn't quite a stranger. Campbell looked up into semi-familiar gray-blue eyes, trying to place where she'd seen this beauty before, but her fuzzy brain couldn't come up with the answer.

"Are you okay?"

The silky voice, the smoldering eyes—the name was on the tip of Campbell's tongue, but even through the haze of her tequila and embarrassment, she knew she'd stared too long. She steadied back into a fully upright position, but kept her hand on the woman's arm more because it felt nice than because she needed the help. "I'm good." She stuck out a hand. "Campbell Clark. I don't usually fall into the arms of women I barely know." She winced at the words, hoping the woman didn't take offense, but also hoping she would respond with an introduction of her own.

The woman gave her a wry smile and reached out to grasp her hand. "Wynne Garrity. And I don't usually stand around in ladies' rooms hoping that women fall into my arms."

Wynne Garrity. The name was familiar, and Campbell was certain if her mind wasn't so muddled, she'd be able to place it. "Me neither," Campbell mumbled, placing her hand over her mouth. "I mean I don't usually fall into women's arms. In restrooms. Or anywhere else for that matter." *Stop talking, stop talking, stop talking.* Campbell straightened her clothes. "Thanks for your help. I'm going to leave now before I say or do any other embarrassing things." She started to walk away, but Wynne's voice stopped her in place.

"You shouldn't be embarrassed."

Campbell turned back around. "Easy for you to say."

Wynne pointed at the corner of the rug which was turned up on itself. "That's an accident waiting to happen. Definitely a dangerous condition." She cocked her head and offered that smile again. "I should think any lawyer would be able to see that."

Thoughts swam through Campbell's head. This woman knew she was a lawyer. Was she at the hotel for the reunion? Campbell struggled to make the connection, mentally flipping through the photos of her graduating class, but before she could place her, Wynne headed to the door.

"If you think you can make it the rest of the way, I've got to go."

Campbell wanted to say "don't," but she couldn't think of a rational reason to ask Wynne to stay. Besides, no matter how much she wanted to, she was in no condition to close the deal on any flirting. "Maybe I'll see you around."

"Maybe."

Wynne tossed the comment over her shoulder as she walked out the door. Campbell stayed in place for a couple of minutes, wondering when she'd lost her finesse. She was going to have to get a lot better at closing deals if she wanted to make her big idea work.

A little while later in the cab, Campbell shot upright, suddenly remembering where she knew Wynne Garrity. She pulled out her phone and opened the Facebook event page for the reunion. The reunion organizers had posted pictures of each of them from their first year in law school. Some of her classmates looked exactly the same now as they had five years ago, but others were now unrecognizable. Campbell scrolled down until she got to the Gs and stilled over a single picture from five years ago. Wynne Garrity fell in the latter group.

Wynne had been the girl in her Con Law class who sat in the front row, prepared to step in whenever whoever was getting the daily grilling couldn't come up with a suitable answer to Professor Lowe's tortuous Socratic method. But unlike the woman she'd just seen, that Wynne hadn't been glamorous. She'd actually been kind of mousy—never one to stand out for anything other than her brain. Campbell had only had the one class with Wynne, which wasn't unusual at a large school like UT, and she didn't remember ever running into her on campus or at the law library where most of their class hung out. They'd never even had a one-on-one conversation. The Wynne she'd just met wasn't anything like the Wynne from law school, but she was intrigued by both versions, and her intrigue almost eclipsed her newfound focus on the fact she was about to quit her job.

Wynne slid behind the wheel of her Honda Accord and leaned back against the seat to catch her breath before starting the engine. She could hardly believe that just a few minutes before she'd been helping the most popular girl in their law school class up off the bathroom floor. But it was true. Campbell Clark, voted by their class as Most Likely to be Everything, had sprawled at her feet in the hotel bathroom.

She shook her head and started the car, wondering if Campbell recognized her. Doubtful. She'd changed a lot in the past five years, and it wasn't like they'd spent any time together over the three years of torture. Wynne had seen Campbell greet her friends across the ballroom this evening, and she'd experienced a tinge of envy that their camaraderie had extended beyond the bounds of their time in law school. Her best friend from school had skipped out on tonight's mixer, and she'd spent most of the night chatting with several of her professors, which wasn't much different from how it had been when she'd been in school. Her law school experience had been very different from Campbell and her friends, and she had nothing in common with them beyond a diploma from UT that said they'd all earned their Juris Doctorate.

The loud ring of her phone startled her out of her musings. She glanced over and smiled at the familiar name displayed on the screen, and then put it on speaker. "Mobile law unit," she said.

"Please send all available units to Worth, Ingram, Nash, and Reed. Stat."

Wynne laughed at the sound of her best friend Seth Greer's voice. "Stat? Uh, I think you're taking the doctor part of Juris Doctor a little too seriously."

"Hell, I need a doctor after the day I've had. Mr. Worth had us working on the Dansen case until five minutes ago. He was drafting anyone in sight to comb through discovery. You missed the perfect opportunity to rack up some hours."

"And you missed watered down drinks and hotel food."

"I've eaten a package of raisins that I found in your desk, so don't even talk about food right now. Or wait, maybe we could dish over pizza. What time should I be at your place?"

Wynne hesitated. Her plan had been to go straight home and get a good night's sleep so she could work tomorrow, but she could use some time to decompress, and the few bites she'd managed to eat tonight were long gone. "Fine, but make the pizza extra crispy. And make my half veggie."

A few minutes later, when she walked through the door of her house, she looked around, but as usual nothing was out of place. Hell, she was barely ever there to mess things up. In the kitchen, she pulled a couple of wine glasses from the cabinet and opened a bottle of red wine to let it breathe or whatever it was that wine did. By the time Seth arrived, she'd changed into jeans and a sweatshirt and felt much more comfortable than she had all evening.

Seth set the pizza on the kitchen counter and reached for the glass she handed to him and took a sip. "This is nice," he said before taking another sip. "Cab?"

She picked up the bottle and read the label. "Blend. A client sent it to Stoltz," she said, referring to her boss. "He prefers Scotch so I wound up with it. His pickiness is your gain."

Seth took another drink. "It's really good. I wish my boss was this generous."

"Generous is probably a strong word," she said with a smile, raising her glass. "He left it in the break room and I snagged it because it looked fancy and I know how you like your expensive wines." She topped off their glasses and they carried the pizza box into the living room and ate directly from it. She raised a slice. "Thanks for this. I didn't realize how hungry I was."

"Try working eighteen hours straight for Mr. Worth, who stayed at the office the entire time to make sure we did everything exactly the way he wanted it. I was all like hey, you've already got your name on the door, who are you trying to impress?"

"You should've come to the reunion," Wynne said. "You could have pitched it as networking."

"Thanks, but no thanks. I do enough fake networking with people I don't know. Besides, I already keep in touch with all the people from school that I want to. No need to wander through a big crowd of assholes I don't remember and who likely don't remember me."

"As if." She wasn't kidding. Seth had been pretty popular in school—not quite as popular as Campbell and her pals—but other students were always seeking him out to be part of their study groups and moot court teams. It was on the tip of her tongue to ask him what he remembered about Campbell, but he interrupted her thoughts with a question of his own.

"Just because I didn't go doesn't mean I don't want to hear all about it. Give me the skinny. Who changed the most and who hasn't changed at all?"

"I ran into Campbell Clark. Do you remember her?"

He munched on his pizza. "Uh-huh. One of the Charlie's Angels."

"What?"

"She and Grace and Abby were inseparable. Just like the Angels, they were always solving cases together, except their mysteries were the cases in law books, unlike the life-and-death cases on the show." He laughed loudly, obviously very amused with himself. When he settled down, he added, "Campbell was the hot one."

"They were all hot," Wynne mused.

"Are we talking movie version or show?"

"Both."

He nodded his approval. "You're right. All the angels were hot. Anyway, she's smart too. I think she works for Hart and Dunn now. How's she doing?"

Wynne had posed her original question to find out what he knew about Campbell, not the other way around. She stalled by gulping the rest of her wine and cycling through potential responses. *She's doing great. Fell right into my arms. Looks like a million bucks. Why do I keep obsessing about this?* She finally settled on, "Good. She's good."

"I always wondered why she went into big law. She's loaded and could do anything she wants."

Loaded, huh? Now there was a piece of gossip about Campbell Clark she didn't know. Figured. Wynne's newfound obsession with Campbell started to recede at learning there was one more thing they didn't have in common. That's okay. She didn't have time to daydream about the Campbell Clarks of the world, or any woman for that matter. Not when she was focused on making partner this year. She pushed away any final thoughts about Campbell's deep red, kissable lips and asked Seth all about his day.

Chapter Three

One month later...

Campbell stood in the center of the newly acquired office space for Clark, Keane, and Maldonado and held her arms over her head and spun around while Abby and Grace watched.

"What are you doing?" Grace asked.

"Soaking it in."

Abby took the spot next to her and raised her arms as well. "Yep, I can feel it too."

Grace tentatively lifted her hands over her head. "What exactly are we feeling?"

"Freedom for one thing," Campbell said. "At no point in the next however long is a partner going to walk through those doors and yell about some research he needs done, or deposition he needs covered, or anything else. No more being sent out to give the client bad news while some partner cowers in their office letting us take the blame for their bad decisions."

"No more jumping through hoops without getting any of the credit," Abby added.

"No more not worrying how the rent gets paid," Grace said. She held up a folder in her hand. "I'd like to call our first meeting, please."

Campbell recognized the tone. It was Grace's let's-get-down-to-business voice, and she remembered it well from their days of studying together in law school. She and Abby had a tendency to start their study sessions with the latest class gossip, but Grace always managed to wrangle them back to the reality of looming exams. Grace's ability to focus on the finer details was precisely why she and Abby had voted to make Grace the managing partner of their fledging firm, and for the past month, Grace had been laser-focused on the millions of details necessary to get their business off the ground. Campbell had a feeling Grace was about to do some financial wrangling, and she was fully prepared to head off any of her concerns. With a flourish, she gestured to the middle of the room. "Shall we sit on the floor and pretend that the pretty new conference table is already here?"

"About that," Grace said, a pained look on her face. "I may have put a hold on the order for the new table."

Campbell cocked her head and squinted at Grace as she parsed her words. "You 'may have put a hold on the order'? What does that mean and why would you do that?" She watched as Grace looked at Abby with a pleading expression, but Abby merely hunched her shoulders. "Would you two like to tell me what's going on?"

Grace sighed and motioned for them to sit. Campbell lowered herself to the floor, glad she'd worn comfortable clothes today. She settled into lotus position and focused on a breathing rhythm she hoped would keep her from whacking someone over the head. When she'd taken a few deep breaths, she turned to face Grace. "Okay, lay it on us. What did you do with the pretty new conference room table?"

"Nothing. I put a hold on it. Just for now. I was thinking maybe we could get something other than a custom piece until we start having a steady cash flow. I saw an ad in the bar journal about a firm that's shutting down and selling off their furniture. They have a nice conference table." She picked up her phone. "I can show you the pics they sent me."

Campbell held up her palm. "Don't need to see them. Let me guess. It's a 'substantial piece' and made of mahogany, cherry, insert some other stodgy heavy wood stain here, and looks pretty much the same as any other conference room table at any other law firm in the country."

"Is there something wrong with that?" Grace asked.

"I thought we all agreed we wanted to show clients our practice is outside the box. Hip, trendy—"

"Frivolous?"

Campbell sighed and turned to Abby for support. After all, the three of them had input into the table design which featured stone from nearby Marble Falls incorporated with sleek modern lines. "You're with me, aren't you, Abby?"

Abby raised her hands in surrender. "I want to be. I absolutely adore the table." She hung her head. "But I'm going to have to side with Grace on this one. Between the rent and all the other things we need—phones, internet, staff—we're kind of bleeding cash until we get some big clients in the door."

"And I'm just saying that in order to get them in the door, we might need to bait the hook."

"Mix your metaphors much?" Grace asked.

"You know what I mean," Campbell said, trying for a measured tone. "If potential clients walk into our conference room and see the same heritage style furnishings as they'd seen at one of our old law firms, then why wouldn't they pick them over us? We need to emphasize the difference between our firm and the firms we came from, not give in to it."

Abby reached over and grasped her arm. "I hear you. I think we all agree, but it's a delicate balance."

"Maybe in a couple of months," Grace added, her tone now contrite. "Once we get some new business in the door, I promise we'll make it a priority."

Campbell twisted her hands as she considered what she was about to say before she plunged in. "I can float us. For a while, I mean. Until we get some cash flow."

"Is that why you were late earlier?" Grace said. "Robbing a bank?"

"You're hilarious." Campbell play punched her. "I got full access to my trust fund this year."

"Oh," Both Abby and Grace said at the same time. "I forgot about that," Abby said. "But don't you want to keep *that* money for...I don't know, something else?"

Campbell should be used to people dancing around the circumstances of her wealth. Hell, she hated talking about it, and there was a time she'd viewed the money from the exorbitant jury award for her parents' wrongful death as blood money that she had no desire to spend. But she liked to think her mom and dad, who'd always supported her dreams, would be happy to see her using the profits from their death for this new venture. "It's not Getty-level money, and I plan to keep most of it for when I'm old and doddering, but there's still plenty to open the firm of our dreams without worrying about going into debt."

"I don't know," Abby said. "It feels like we'd be starting out not on an even playing field between the three of us. Grace, what do you think?"

Campbell held her breath, pretty sure Grace would be the first one to speak up in opposition.

"Well, I'd definitely prefer to find the funds another way, but if Campbell wants to loan the firm some seed money, it's not a terrible idea. My primary concern is making sure we don't make any decisions about money that could affect our power dynamic, let alone our friendship. How about we keep it in reserve for now, and revisit it in a month or two when we have a better idea of where things stand?"

Fair and rational. Trademark Grace. Campbell nodded. "Good plan. But in the meantime, I'm making an executive decision and paying for the new conference table. Consider it my gift to all of us for taking this leap. Besides, if I have to see the same old stodgy furniture every day, then I may as well go back to work for Hart and Dunn aka Stodgy and Boring, LLP."

"Deal," Abby said, quickly followed by Grace who smiled her assent.

Satisfied they'd reached an acceptable compromise, Campbell said, "Now that that's settled, I have a lunch date with my brother to try to drum up some business. Doors open in one week, ladies!"

❖

Wynne pushed aside some papers on her desk and sighed when a stack fell to the floor. When she reached down to pick them up, she spotted a copy of the program from her law school reunion weekend in the mix, and she flipped it open. She'd thought about the reunion—make that her brush with Campbell Clark—several times over the past month, but she'd resisted the urge to Google Campbell or otherwise dwell on why she cared to know more about her.

"Wynne?"

Startled, Wynne dropped the program back on the floor as the secretary she shared with the senior litigation partner appeared in her doorway. "Hey, Jennifer, what's up?"

"He wants to see you. And yes, I told him you were headed to the Wilson meeting."

"It's okay." It wasn't, but there was nothing Wynne could do about it. "He" was Jerry Stoltz, the senior partner in their division at Worth, Ingram, Nash, and Reed, and when he called, everyone jumped. Everyone who wanted to make partner anyway. Failure to respond to Stoltz's call would outweigh all the extra billable hours she'd managed to rack up over the last five years. Hours that had resulted in big end of year bonuses, bonuses that had gone straight into safe investment accounts, but would disappear quickly if she didn't have the security of her job.

She quickly gathered the files she'd need for the deposition and shoved them into her bag. On her way to Stoltz's office, she dropped her stuff at Jennifer's desk and told her she'd be right back for it. When she approached Stoltz's office, she paused to listen to him railing at someone, but she couldn't tell if his rant was directed at someone inside or on the phone. She knocked on the door, knowing he wouldn't appreciate her attempt to be considerate by waiting until he was done. Stoltz didn't value politeness, especially not at the office. To him, courtesy was a waste of time, and time was money.

"Come in," he barked.

She opened the door and tiptoed into the room, spotting Stoltz behind his desk with the phone in one hand and a Red Bull in the other. He jabbed his finger at a spot behind her before resuming his conversation on the phone, and she quietly shut the door. She remained standing and pretended not to listen to his conversation, but she was totally soaking up every word.

"The kid is crazy," Stoltz growled into the phone. "Sure, he came up with the original idea, but it's not his smarts that make money. You need to get him under control…I know, I know, but I'm tired of getting texts from him every two seconds, telling me I'm behind the times. When did clients start thinking it was okay to text anyway?"

Shortly after dinosaurs stopped roaming the earth. Wynne focused on using one of the breathing exercises she'd learned from Seth to keep her growing angst at bay, but she'd barely managed to count to eight when Stoltz slammed down the phone.

"Have a seat," he said in a remarkably calm voice.

Despite his apparent frustration at whoever had been on the other end of the phone, it didn't seem to be spilling over onto her. She wanted to tell him she didn't have time to sit down since the meeting he'd scheduled and commanded her to handle was supposed to start seconds from now, but she knew it would be an exercise in futility. She'd barely settled in one of the chairs across from his gargantuan desk before he launched in.

"Braxton Keith is a menace."

Ah, that explained the phone call, and now Wynne knew exactly which client Stoltz had been complaining about. Braxton

Keith, twenty-something whiz kid, was probably the youngest business client of the firm, and his youthful enthusiasm for his internet start-up Leaderboard, and all things technological, spilled over into every interaction he had with his lawyers. Stoltz hated him. Actually, hate was a strong word. It was probably more like he viewed Brax—their client insisted everyone call him by the shortened version of his name—as an entitled child who wanted his lawyers to bless all his business transactions no matter how impractical and irresponsible they might be. Wynne didn't particularly like the guy, but she respected his smarts and insight into the future of social media. Menace wasn't the word she would have used, but there really wasn't an appropriate comment to make in response to Stoltz's assessment, so she bided her time, knowing from experience Stoltz didn't need anyone else's contribution to make a conversation. "Uh-hmm," she said, careful to keep her tone neutral.

"His new venture's barely been in place for six months and already he's getting smacked with a big lawsuit from some two-bit singer, Rhea Hendricks."

Wynne resisted pointing out that Rhea Hendricks was an up-and-coming country music powerhouse. "Leaderboard?"

"What?"

Wynne cursed herself for speaking up, but now that she had, she treaded carefully. "The venture? Was it the Leaderboard app?"

Stoltz made a show of looking for something on his desk. "Yes, I think that was it. No one even understands how it works, so how did they manage to find a cause of action against it?"

Wynne let the rhetorical question go. She understood the basics of how Leaderboard worked, but since Stoltz relied on her to do just that, he wouldn't want to be reminded that her comprehension of Brax's premier product exceeded his. "What can I do to help?"

Stoltz stopped fussing with the papers on his desk and smiled, not a friendly smile, but a feral curling of the lips, and Wynne braced for impact. "Word on the street is that Braxton is hunting around for a new law firm," Stoltz said. "His board has no desire to switch, but they are also tired of dealing with his temper tantrums when he doesn't get his way. Go make nice with Braxton and keep him in the fold. He wants someone to make this litigation go away without any effort. I need you to impress upon him the importance of getting out in front and squashing the plaintiff like a bug. Jennifer has a copy of the plaintiff's complaint for you. Finish the meeting with Wilson today, and then everything else takes a back burner to Braxton Keith. You keep him happy and I will take care of you. Understood?"

She understood perfectly. She'd still be responsible for her regular caseload, but Brax was now her number one priority. It was going to be hard to juggle everything, but if babysitting Braxton Keith was her key to partnership, she wasn't about to blow it. "Understood."

She ducked out of his office and grabbed her bag from Jennifer's desk. "J, will you set up a meeting for me at Braxton's Meadow's office? As soon as he's available." She paused for a second. "Once you've got it set up, see if one of the new kids are available to go with," she said, referring to the crop of law school students doing their summer internship at the firm. "There's one with a tech background. Sorry, I don't remember his name."

"On it," Jennifer said, scribbling a note. "I've called ahead to let them know you were delayed. If you leave now, you won't be too late."

"I'm already gone," Wynne called out as she ran for the elevator. The meeting was being held at opposing counsel's office down the street so at least she wouldn't have to fight traffic to get there. Despite her hurry, when she pushed through the lobby doors, she couldn't help but pause and soak in the beautiful spring day. After a solid month of March rain, the bright sun was a welcome change even if it was likely to turn into a burning circle of hell by

June. Nothing she could do about that but enjoy the good weather while she could, and by enjoy she meant catch a moment here and there between bouts of work. She thought back to seeing Campbell Clark and her pals at the reunion, laughing like they didn't have a care in the world, and wondered what that would be like. She shrugged. No sense wondering about things that were never going to happen.

Chapter Four

Campbell tapped her fingers on the table and looked around the restaurant patio. She loved every single thing on the menu at Moonshine Grill, and it didn't help that she was starving. If her brother, Justin, didn't show up soon, she was going to order one of everything and stick him with the bill. To distract her desire to eat all the things, she replayed the conversation she'd just had with Grace and Abby in her head. In her opinion, the whole money thing was a distraction. She totally got how they would prefer that the firm pay its own way, but new businesses borrowed money all the time. They could go to the bank and take out a loan, or save the exorbitant interest rate and let her finance their start-up costs. Her way was clearly better overall—she just needed to find a way to convince Grace it wouldn't affect their relationship.

"Sorry I'm late."

Campbell looked up at her tall, slim brother, struck as usual by how much he looked like their father. She wondered if his hair would gray early like Dad's had. Justin had earned the gray after taking care of her and their younger sister, Perry, after their parents' death. The memory of the three of them, holding hands and standing graveside at the double funeral, clouded her thoughts, and she shook her head to clear away the image. "Words aren't going to cut it, bro. You're buying."

"You may change your tune when you hear my news."

She motioned to his chair. "Sit and tell all." She picked up the menu. "But first I'm going to order everything on here." She waved to the waiter and, after Justin nodded for her to go ahead, she ordered their favorites. As soon as the waiter walked away, she crossed her hands on the table. "Spill."

"You've heard of Braxton Keith?"

"Of course. Founder of Leaderboard and featured in last month's *Rolling Stone*. Wasn't he also at South by Southwest?"

"Exactly. He was rolling out some new developments for the Leaderboard app."

"Right. The Hunger Games of social media."

"Maybe, but the IPO is expected to be priced at over seventy bucks a share."

Campbell whistled low. The initial offering probably made her trust fund look like peanuts. "That's insane."

"Agreed, but not all is well in Braxton's world. He may be looking for a new law firm."

Campbell scooted to the edge of her seat. "And I have a new law firm."

"Exactly. That's what I told him."

"Wait, what? When did you meet Braxton Keith?"

"At South by Southwest. My group was doing a showcase about some add-on software we've developed for apps like Leaderboard, and he stopped by to ask some questions about it. Everyone was super starstruck, but he and I hit it off and had some beers after. A few drinks in, he started griping about how the law firm his board hired are a bunch of stick-in-the-muds who barely even know how to use modern technology let alone know how to represent the guy on the cutting edge of it."

"Hold up. You had beers with the Braxton Keith? Like for real?"

Justin grinned. "You hold up. He's just a guy. A brilliant and pretty arrogant guy, but he's not a superhero or anything."

"He's the lord of the internet and he's a billionaire."

"Little b billionaire, but yes, he has earned a billion since Leaderboard launched. But he mentioned they are starting to draw some lawsuits. The law firm they've been using is big on settling cases instead of going to trial, and he thinks it's because they don't understand how the site works or its significance. You understand how Leaderboard works, right?"

"Sure," Campbell said, faking confidence she didn't feel. She was on Leaderboard, but mostly because everyone else was, but she hadn't taken time to figure out how to game the system to rise in the ranks. Besides, when it first came out, so many people were predicting it would be a flash in the pan. Except Abby. Abby was really into it. She made a mental note to call Abby as soon as lunch was over.

"I know that look," Justin said. "It's the 'I'll fake it until I can get to Google and look up what I need to know look.'"

"Maybe I could use a refresher."

He rolled his eyes and pulled out his phone. "Here's the crash course. It's a lot like all the other popular social media sites, but there's kind of a competition angle to it because you can accumulate points. You create a profile and you get points for how much information you provide. That's your base score and you need to score the minimum to even get on the board."

"So long privacy."

"And welcome to transparency. No Russian bots here." He pointed to his own profile. "The goal really is transparency, so you know who you're connecting with."

"Makes sense. Keep talking."

"There's not a lot more to it. To rise in rank on the board, you need to earn more points by connecting and engaging with other people, but the goal is quality connections, not just quantity."

"And how in the world is that measured?"

"That's the magic. Brax has developed an algorithm to measure the quality, but basically the higher the quality of your interactions and connections, the higher you rise on the boards. For example if you post a meme and a hundred people like it, that's good, but you'll get even more points if people comment on the meme and then those people comment on each other's comments. If you get well-known people, aka leaders, to comment, then you score even higher. The formula is pretty complex and it's all very proprietary."

"What's he getting sued for?"

"Hell if I know. I only know he doesn't care for his current law firm, which is where you come in."

"So me, you, and Brax are going to meet up, have drinks, and he'll hire Clark, Keane, and Maldonado to do all his legal work?"

"Maybe."

"Explain to me again how you and the Brax became such good friends that you could help me land a pitch with his company?"

Justin shrugged. "What can I say? The guy knows talent when he sees it." He pointed at his own chest. "Exhibit A. And I have no doubt that he will believe Exhibit B," he pointed at Campbell, "being of the same bloodline of the House of Clark must also possess talent."

"When you go full-on nerd, I know you're really serious." The waiter appeared with their food and Campbell dove into the fries. "My little golden stick of joy!" she exclaimed before biting into the crispy potato. "Oh, how I've missed you."

"You must never abandon the golden stick of joy," Justin proclaimed in his best *Game of Thrones* voice while waving a fry in the air. "Only woe comes to those to travel such a path."

"Oh, trust me, now that we're past the reunion, I'm back on fries." Campbell munched another few to emphasize her point.

"How was the reunion? You know, besides you, Grace, and Abby deciding to quit your jobs?"

"You make it sound like we formed a cult."

"Most people go to reunions to show off where they are in life, but you three…" He shook his head.

"I know, I know. It seems crazy, but seriously, it was the best thing I've ever done." Campbell contemplated his original question. "The reunion was fun. A lot of people came in from out of town, and it was nice to see people I hadn't seen in a while. I mean, it's a big school, but everyone had a core group they hung out with, and after spending three years in each other's business, five years apart made it feel like we hadn't seen each other in forever." For some reason Campbell's mind wandered off as she was talking. Who was Wynne's core group? She remembered she'd hung out with Seth Greer most of the time, but she didn't recall seeing her around the common areas all that much. Wynne had taken some of the top honors in their class—she remembered that much from graduation—but she didn't have a clue where Wynne had gone to work after graduation. Had she stayed in Austin? What kind of law did she practice?

More importantly, why did she care?

Because she felt a twinge of something the night she'd run into Wynne in the bathroom at the reunion. *You probably just felt her pity because you couldn't manage to stand upright.*

No, it was something more than that. She hadn't gotten the impression Wynne had been judging her. It was almost like Wynne had wanted to talk, to connect. Maybe she'd imagined it, but she didn't think so. More importantly, why did it matter?

"Look sharp, sis. Guess who's headed our way?"

Campbell shook away her mixed-up feelings about Wynne Garrity and glanced in the direction Justin was not so subtlety jerking his chin to see none other than Braxton Keith headed their way, a huge grin on his face. To Campbell's surprise, he actually stopped at their table and clasped her brother on the shoulder.

"Justin Clark." Braxton clasped Justin's hand. "Great to see you, bro."

Campbell watched while Justin engaged in a surreal conversation with one of the most up-and-coming entrepreneurs in the country, and she took the time to assess Braxton up close. With his youthful looks, anyone passing him on the street would assume he was one of the many college students at UT, and his choice of clothing—Whiskey Shivers T-shirt, Chucks, and jeans—supported that assumption. She knew from the *Rolling Stone* article he was a twenty-seven-year-old graduate of MIT. Not a child prodigy by any means, but way more successful than most people her age. Including her. Of course that could change if she could win his business.

"Brax, meet my sister Campbell. Campbell is one of the founding partners of Clark, Keane, and Maldonado, a cutting edge law firm here in town."

Brax turned his winning smile on her, and Campbell spotted curiosity in his eyes. She stuck out a hand. "Nice to meet the guy who's turning social media into a gamer's sport."

His slow nod showed his respect for her assessment. "You a gamer?"

She wanted to say yes, but suspected Brax wasn't someone to bullshit. Besides she could only speak the language for a few minutes before he'd figure out she was bluffing. "No, but when you grow up with a brother who writes them, you get honorary status. But I don't have to be a gamer to appreciate Leaderboard." Deciding she had nothing to lose, she pulled out a card and handed it over. "I hope everyone you have on your team appreciates your expertise."

He glanced at the card and then tapped it on the table before slipping it into his pocket. "We should talk. Later. Right now I have a meeting." His grimace said how much he was looking forward to it. "I'll text you."

"Perfect." Campbell met his big smile with one of her own and waited until he was several feet away from the table to look at Justin.

"Bold move, sis."

"Fortune favors the bold."

"Yeah, don't talk like that when you meet with him. You sound like a history teacher."

"I'm working on my very best nerd."

"That's the thing. Nerds don't want to hire nerds to represent them. They want lawyers who can communicate with the rest of the world on their behalf."

"Got it. Hide the nerd gene." Campbell looked across the patio where Brax was standing in front of another table. "He actually looks like a cool guy."

"I'm guessing it's partly an act. He's dressed like a hipster because that's what investors expect." Justin followed her gaze. "I bet he's meeting with some investors right now."

Just then a woman seated at the table where Brax had stopped stood up and shook his hand and motioned for him to have a seat. There was nothing remarkable about the exchange except that the woman was Wynne Garrity, and she looked devastatingly beautiful in a sharply tailored black suit. How had she gone the five years since graduation without seeing Wynne and then run into her twice within a month? And more importantly, what was Wynne doing having lunch with Braxton Keith?

Wynne typed a quick email on her phone and then glanced at the menu. The thought of the big pile of work waiting for her back at the office robbed her appetite, and she couldn't help but be annoyed Braxton had insisted they meet at a restaurant instead of at his office.

"What's the matter?"

She looked over at the intern, Daniel, who'd tagged along for the meeting, surprised at the question. She needed to get her game face on. If he could tell she wasn't happy, Braxton would probably notice too. All she needed was for Braxton to report to Stoltz one more reason he was dissatisfied with the firm, and then Stoltz would blame her if they lost Leaderboard's business. "Not a thing. Just trying to decide between the chicken sandwich and a salad."

He nodded, none the wiser. "I'm having the ribs," he announced, setting aside his menu and folding his hands on the table as if his lunch choice was all the work he needed to do today.

Wynne shoved the menu back in front of him. "Pick again, big shot. Braxton Keith is a billionaire, but he doesn't eat meat. You can, but nothing that's going to gross him out like a bunch of bones on your plate. Also, don't order anything that will take long to prepare. He doesn't like to wait around." She watched Daniel frown and then reluctantly reopen his menu to scan the choices. Normally she wouldn't care if an intern wanted to make a fool of himself by taking advantage of the firm expense account and gnawing on messy food, but she needed Braxton to like this guy because Daniel spoke Braxton's language—geek speak.

"Did you review the complaint?" she asked.

"Yes," Daniel said, straightening up in his chair.

"Great. Tell me the primary causes of action Hendricks is alleging."

Daniel cast a wistful glance at the menu and set it aside. "She's got the usual fluff claims, fraud, intentional infliction of emotional distress, breach of contract, but she's also alleged business disparagement. The big one is tortious interference with prospective business relations."

"And what facts does Hendricks allege to support that one?" Wynne already knew the answer, but part of her job was to teach the summer interns, and she was curious to see if Daniel had done his homework.

"Hendricks has been trying to cross over from music to film for a while, and last year she was up for the lead in a feature film about Joan Baez, but she lost the part when her Leaderboard ranking tanked shortly after her engagement to Dash Wilder fell apart. Wilder has a top tier ranking on Leaderboard and a bunch of his connections severed ties with her after the breakup. Basically, she blames Leaderboard, specifically Braxton Keith, for all her troubles."

Speaking of Braxton, where the hell was he? Wynne glanced around and then spotted him standing across the room, chatting with a couple who were seated on the other side of the patio, looking like he had all the time in the world. Technically, he did because she was definitely billing for this, at four hundred dollars an hour. A few minutes later, after she'd listened to Daniel change his mind a half dozen times about what he planned to order, Braxton finally headed their way. She stood as he approached the table and motioned for Daniel to do the same, annoyed at his lack of manners. Hell, she sounded like a little old lady.

"Wynne, sorry I'm late. I ran into a friend, and…"

He kept talking, but she didn't hear him because her gaze was firmly fixed on a face across the room. The woman had had her back to her when she'd been seated and talking to Braxton, but now that she'd stood up and her profile was in full view, there was no denying the familiar face. It was Campbell Clark.

"Have you already ordered?"

Braxton's voice cut through her foggy brain, and she willed the cloud of Campbell to clear. "Yes. I mean, no, we waited for you. Your secretary said you love this place." She pointed at the menu, resisting the urge to look in Campbell's direction again. "Any recommendations?"

Braxton shoved his menu to the side. "Actually, I like to come here for the patio. I'm going to have a salad, but order whatever you want."

Wynne heard Daniel sigh, and she nudged him under the table and gave him a quick shake of her head. "We were just looking at the menu. Shall I order three of the house salads?"

"Sounds great," Braxton said, setting aside his menu. Wynne shot Daniel a stern look, daring him to challenge her decision, but he simply handed her his menu and echoed Braxton's words.

Their salads were delivered quickly, and over the next forty-five minutes, Braxton insisted on talking about everything except Leaderboard or the pending litigation. Wynne bit her tongue and went with the flow, certain that Braxton would rebel if she tried to steer the conversation in a particular direction. Daniel didn't seem to care at all, content to swap stories with Braxton about the last sci-fi con he'd attended and the amazing new games he'd had a chance to test drive. For a few minutes, Wynne even zoned out, her mind drifting back to the Campbell Clark sighting. Campbell was no longer on the patio, but Wynne wanted to know why she'd been talking to Braxton in the first place. Was their acquaintance personal or professional? Unlikely it was professional considering Worth Ingram did all the legal work for Braxton's enterprises, a representation envied by all the top firms in Austin, likely Campbell's as well.

She'd Googled Campbell after the reunion. Campbell had done quite well for herself. She was a fifth-year associate at Hart and Dunn, and she'd been active with the local bar and the state organization of young lawyers. Wynne wasn't sure why she was surprised at Campbell's accomplishments. People like Campbell usually cruised to success on their charm and good looks, while people like her had to claw their way there.

Speaking of clawing, she realized she better get Braxton to focus on the lawsuit against Leaderboard or she'd have nothing to report to Stoltz when she got back to the office. She let a few beats pass after the waiter cleared their plates before treading carefully into a more substantive conversation. "Brax, we have a couple of upcoming deadlines we need to discuss in the Rhea Hendricks case." No sooner had she spoken the plaintiff's name than she felt him tense and stiffen.

Brax shrugged. "She'll go away. Nothing more than a disgruntled diva."

"That may be true. Eventually. But the fact that she filed a lawsuit is a clear sign that it's going to take some work to get that to happen."

"And let me guess, lots of billable hours." He waved a fork between her and Daniel. "You're both billing for this lunch, right?" Before she could answer, he added, "And I appreciate that you brought this kid along to soften me up with his whole gamer vibe, but I don't think you people understand where I'm coming from. I don't need you to know every little thing about my business, but I do need you to care about it as much as I do, so you can protect me from people who will try to destroy what I've built. That means I need to see some passion. I need to feel like you're really on my side and not just viewing these lawsuits like a cash cow. You should know that Worth Ingram was not my choice, and if the board hadn't picked your firm, we wouldn't be sitting here today. Jerry Stoltz doesn't know the first thing about how Leaderboard works, and I doubt he even cares. He thinks I'm some jerk kid who made too much money too fast and probably deserves to get sued."

Well, that was a lot to unpack. Wynne took a deep breath before diving in. "I think you're brilliant. And no, I'm not just blowing smoke up your ass. I understand how Leaderboard works, and that's why I'm working on your case." She pointed at Daniel. "Daniel here is an intern. Part of how we become a top-notch law firm is to find the best talent and groom young lawyers by letting them participate in groundbreaking work. In addition to law, Daniel has a special interest in all things tech, so I brought him along, not only because I thought he would speak your language, but as a benefit to his real world education. We are not billing for his time at this lunch." She purposely didn't look at Daniel as she spoke, knowing her last pronouncement would shock him. "No matter who made the decision to hire us, the intent was the same—protect your interests, right?"

"Yes, but—"

She cut Braxton off, hoping she wouldn't regret it later. "Then let us do what we know is best. You have experience with programming and building a business from the ground up. We have experience and expertise in helping our clients keep what's theirs and not letting anyone interfere with their success. Rhea Hendricks is an interference. Let us do what we do best and neutralize her. But I can promise you this—ignoring her will not achieve that."

Brax looked like he wanted to protest, but she kept a level stare at him, daring him to challenge her and hoping he wouldn't call her bluff.

"I guess you're right."

It wasn't a ringing endorsement, but it would have to do for now because Wynne knew she'd pushed him as far as she could without risking losing his business. "I'll show you that we are. Just give me a chance."

At that moment, the waiter showed back up with the bill, and Wynne grabbed it before Brax could. "I've got this, and no, it won't show up on your next statement." She produced her firm credit card and waited for the waiter to withdraw before making the pitch she'd come here to discuss. "I promise we won't get in the way of your business, but it would be really helpful for our initial answer to the lawsuit and discovery to have a sit-down with anyone who worked on the Leaderboard algorithms. The sooner the better."

Brax was already out of his seat. "I hear you. Let me talk to my team and I'll be in touch. I promise I'll get back to you before the end of the week."

Wynne watched him leave certain she'd blown the meeting, but not at all sure what she could've done differently to win him over. She recognized Brax's vague "I'll be in touch" for the delay tactic it was. Could Stoltz be right? Was Brax really considering ditching the firm to hire someone else to take over? It was hard to believe he'd sever ties with them so soon, but he struck her as the impatient type, unlikely to want to wait for the firm to catch up to him.

The image of Campbell shaking Brax's hand flooded her awareness. Had Campbell been at the restaurant today to meet with Brax? Was Hart and Dunn vying for his business? The idea that they'd schedule a meeting right in front of her seemed ludicrous, but she wasn't ready to dismiss it completely. Hart and Dunn had a good reputation in the Austin tech community, and they had the resources to handle top tier litigation.

"Are you ready?" Daniel asked, already out of his chair.

Good question, she thought, wondering if she was indeed ready to do battle to keep Brax's business. She'd worked hard to help Braxton launch his success, and she wasn't about to cede her position as counselor to anyone else, especially not an all fluff, no substance lawyer like Campbell Clark. She stood and led the way to the car. She was ready to do battle to keep her client, and nothing and no one was going to get in the way.

Chapter Five

Campbell burst into Grace's office after lunch, only to find her on the phone. She paced in the doorway for a few moments before she motioned to Grace to join her and Abby in the conference room when she finished the call.

"What's all the fuss?" Abby asked as she took a seat.

"Wait until Grace is here."

"Sounds mysterious."

Campbell merely nodded. She'd barely been able to contain her excitement since she'd met Braxton Keith at lunch. She'd gone directly from the restaurant to the nearest coffee shop and spent the last hour sketching out some notes about how to win Leaderboard's business. Her brainstorming had been interrupted by a text from Braxton, and now it was time for a brainstorming session with Grace and Abby to round out her plan.

"I'm guessing lunch went well," Abby said.

Campbell opened her mouth to say that she wasn't going to let Abby pry it out of her, but Grace burst into the conference room at that moment.

"Thank God you're here," Abby said. "I can't get her to tell me a thing."

"I wanted you both to hear the good news at the same time."

"Good news?" Grace said, her eyes bright with hope. "I love good news."

"I know you do, and that is why I'm happy to say that we have a meeting with Braxton Keith. Tomorrow."

"Wait, what?" Abby leaned forward. "Was that the business Justin was drumming up for you? How does he know Braxton? It's impossible to get a meeting with him."

Campbell held up her cell. "Not impossible. It's a done deal. The meeting anyway. We get one shot to convince him to ditch his current law firm." She set the phone on the conference table, turned it so they could read the screen, and watched Grace scroll through the text exchange she'd since memorized.

Cool meeting you. Might be looking for new lawyer. Interested?

Definitely. I think we'd be a perfect fit.

Board meeting tomorrow. I'll send you some papers to review. See you at nine a.m., Leaderboard HQ.

We'll be there.

Grace looked up from the phone. "Wow."

"I know," Campbell said. "I get it's not a lot of time to prepare, but look at it this way, we'll be fresh."

"What are the papers he's sending?"

"Sent." Campbell reached into a box by her chair and pulled out copies to pass around. "Leaderboard is being sued by country music's very own Rhea Hendricks. She claims she lost a role in an upcoming Joan Baez biopic because her ranking fell between the time she entered talks with the studio and the time to ink the deal. Claims they yanked it from her and gave it to whatshername, that chick whose ranking soared when it came out that she was sleeping with that guy who was the first runner-up on *The Bachelor.*"

"Are you speaking English right now?" Grace asked.

"Oops, I forgot your aversion to reality TV."

Abby tapped her phone. "Plus, Grace isn't on Leaderboard."

"Grace isn't only not on Leaderboard, Grace isn't sure what Leaderboard is," Grace said.

Campbell gave them the breakdown Justin had given her. "So, basically it's all driven by an algorithm that's proprietary. If Brax has to disclose anything about the development and use of the algorithm, then anyone can use it to develop their own program and his business will crater, which makes him extra cautious about how this case is handled."

"Brax, huh?" Abby said. "How did you happen to meet him?"

"Justin met him at a South by Southwest session, and they hit it off. Now they're bros and we have a way into the kingdom that is Leaderboard Inc."

"Who's their current law firm?" Grace asked.

"Worth Ingram. I get the impression he's not impressed with their grasp of the coolness factor of his platform, and it may be they don't even understand its potential. Anyway, he's not happy with them. He told Justin, Justin arranged for us to meet, and the rest is history."

"History in the making," Grace said. "If we're going to put on a show for the board meeting tomorrow, we're going to have to work all night. Let's make a list of what needs to be done and split up tasks." She didn't wait for an answer before she started jotting notes. Campbell loved that about her. Grace might be a bit more practical than she liked, but she could be counted on to organize like a boss, and Campbell was happy to let her be in control of that part of the process.

Abby punched the keys of her laptop. "I just downloaded the docket sheet for the lawsuit. Looks like they're still in the really early phases. The lead attorney for Leaderboard is one of the partners at Worth Ingram. Jerry Stoltz."

"I know him," Campbell said. "We were up against their firm last year in a product liability case. He's an ass. An old school ass at that. Brought a bunch of first year lawyers to all the depositions with him to act as his own personal entourage. I bet his monthly billing to Leaderboard is astronomical."

"I'll start reviewing the pleadings and make a run at creating a defense strategy," Abby said.

"I'll put together an initial budget," Grace said. "It's going to be loose without knowing a bunch more details, like how many witnesses on either side, etc., but I have no doubt we could come in under whatever Worth Ingram is charging."

"Let's float some flat fee options," Campbell added. "And maybe a hybrid flat fee and hourly rate. I'm sure Worth is charging at least three fifty an hour, and they'll never go for a flat fee. If we get this lawsuit, we have a chance at getting all of Leaderboard's business."

Grace made a note. "Good plan. On it." She looked up from her notes. "And you're in for the big presentation, right?"

Campbell smiled. All three of them were smart, but they each had specific strengths. Abby was the brilliant legal mind, Grace was the brilliant businessperson, and her job? Well, she was the front woman, the put-on-a-show and convince a client that not hiring them would be the biggest mistake of their lives. She loved the pressure of coming up with a personalized presentation, but she wasn't sure she'd ever had less than twenty-four hours to do so. She mustered confidence she didn't quite feel and announced, "On it."

❖

"What happened at lunch?" Jennifer asked as Wynne walked past her desk.

Wynne paused. She could tell Jennifer was worried, but she wasn't sure how to answer. Lunch had been hours ago. She'd gone straight from there to another client's office to interview a witness. "Nothing bad. At least I didn't think so. What's up?"

"Not sure, but there's a board meeting at Leaderboard tomorrow, and Braxton called to say he wants a presentation on the status of the case. I went ahead and moved around your appointments so you can make it."

"Won't he want Stoltz instead?"

Jennifer glanced at her boss's office door and dropped her voice to a whisper. "He specifically said he wants you to give the presentation."

A loud voice bellowed through Jennifer's phone intercom. "Is she back yet?"

Knowing she was the "she" he was referring to, Wynne motioned to Stoltz's door. "I got this."

A moment later, she was standing in front of Stoltz's desk, hoping that by not sitting down she could make this meeting as short as possible.

"I need to know everything that was said at this little meeting you had with Braxton."

Wynne heard his derisive tone and resisted the urge to point out he'd forced her to have the meeting, sending her rather than going himself, but instead she cut to the chase. "He thinks we're antiquated and not capable of understanding the worth of Leaderboard. He thinks that mindset will negatively affect how we handle this case, and he's worried we won't adequately protect his interests."

"He told you all that?"

"Not word for word, but that's basically the gist of what he had to say."

"Well, that's ridiculous. It's pretty clear you bungled the meeting. Didn't I tell you to meet with him and soothe him over?" He waved her off. "Never mind. I'll show up tomorrow and have a few choice words with the board. Thankfully, there are cooler, wiser heads responsible for the company than that hotshot who thinks he knows everything."

Wynne had a vision of Stoltz schooling the board while Brax seethed in the background. The board might ultimately elect to stick with their counsel, but their relationship with Brax would be permanently damaged, which would make it impossible to provide him with effective representation. It would only be a matter of time before he figured out how to ditch them. She had to find a way to compromise Stoltz's desire to put the kid in his place and their need to keep Leaderboard's business, because if the business went away, she was certain Stoltz would lay the blame on her. Bye-bye partnership.

An hour later, she snuck away to the break room for some much needed coffee and ran into Seth.

"Hey, stranger," he said. "Someone's been busy lately."

"Don't even. Busy isn't the word I'd use to describe the whirlwind around here."

He handed her a mug from the cabinet and, without having to ask, popped her favorite K-cup in the Keurig. "Please tell me something to take my mind off the mind-numbing interrogatories I'm having to comb through since the new crop of associates is too busy studying for the bar exam to be bothered helping me out."

Wynne looked back over her shoulder and, satisfied no partners were in sight, recounted the details of her lunch with Braxton.

"And he just left things like that?"

"That's how Braxton is. I can't tell if it's an eccentricity or if he just likes to keep people guessing." The Keurig sputtered the last few drops into her cup and she reached for it like a lifeline. "Whatever's going on, it's keeping me here all night because suddenly we've been called on the carpet." She took a sip. "Board meeting tomorrow at Leaderboard."

"Agenda?"

"'A report on the case,' but who knows? I'll plan for everything and see what happens. Stoltz says he's going to do all the talking."

"Oh, that'll win them over for sure." Seth's voice was laced with sarcasm. "I don't have anything going on tonight. Can I help?"

For a second, Wynne considered taking him up on it. They rarely had the chance to work together, and the prospect of a late night cram session with him brought back memories of pulling all-nighters before exams. But she needed to work from the office, and if Stoltz saw her pulling in another senior associate to help, he'd view it as a weakness. She'd put a few of the junior associates to work and do the heavy lifting on her own. "I'm good with this stuff, but I do have a question about something slightly related."

Seth leaned in. "Spill."

"You've got a pal who works at Hart and Dunn, right?" At his nod, she continued. "Have you heard any rumors that they're making a bid for Leaderboard's business?"

He shook his head. "What makes you think that's a possibility?"

"Today at lunch, Braxton stopped to chat with some guy I'd never seen before and Campbell Clark was sitting at the table with him. And Braxton's definitely unhappy with Stoltz. The timing has me thinking that maybe Hart and Dunn is making a move on Leaderboard."

Seth laughed. "That sounds so dirty. But I don't think you saw what you thought you did. I guess you haven't heard. Campbell Clark quit her job at Hart and Dunn. Not too long after the reunion in fact. She and Grace and Abby are starting their own firm. I don't even think they're up and running yet. I heard about it from my pal that works at Hart at the last ABA happy hour…"

Seth kept talking about other gossip he'd learned while drinking with his pals, but Wynne was playing catch-up, struggling to process his news. Campbell was in her fifth year with Hart and Dunn, likely on the same kind of partnership track as she was. Had Campbell seriously given up that kind of tenure to strike out on her own? What was it like to be able to throw your career progress to the wind and start over? Wynne shuddered at the idea of giving up everything she'd worked so hard to earn and start from scratch. Definitely not a path she was interested in taking, but why did she care that Campbell had?

She didn't. Campbell Clark and her career weren't any concern of hers. Especially now that she knew Campbell wasn't competition for Leaderboard's business. No way could a fledging firm of three lawyers provide the level of legal services that Leaderboard's business demanded.

Later that night in her office, she took a break from preparing for tomorrow's board meeting and let her fingers stray over the keyboard of her computer. The very first item returned on her Google search was an announcement in the local bar journal heralding the formation of Clark, Keane, and Maldonado. Before she could think about the rabbit hole she was plunging into, Wynne clicked on the link and read the short announcement, and then clicked on the link to the new firm's website, and then clicked on the link for Campbell's bio. And then she stopped clicking, mesmerized by Campbell Clark's caramel eyes staring back into hers with searing intensity. Campbell was stylish and beautiful and completely captivating. And it took every bit of Wynne's willpower to close the website and get back to work.

Chapter Six

Campbell leaned across the console of the car and pointed to the sign up ahead. "Turn left into the parking lot. Right there." She jabbed her finger at the window. "You're going to miss it."

Grace smacked her hand away. "Stop it. I know where I'm going. Aren't you supposed to be concentrating on the pitch?"

Campbell started to spout off a sharp retort, but Abby's hand on her shoulder stopped her.

"We got this," Abby said, her voice sure and calm.

"Sorry," Campbell said, wishing she was as relaxed as Abby seemed. "This is a big deal."

"It is a big deal, but Abby's right," Grace said. "We got this. We're as prepared as we could possibly be, and you'll be your usual rock star self once you get started."

Grace was right, at least about the prepared part. Between the three of them, they'd managed to put together a sleek presentation that was custom-tailored to Braxton Keith and his board. Abby had prepared an interactive multimedia presentation, and Grace had thoroughly researched every one of the board members so they could incorporate key points that would touch on their individual concerns. While the overall composition of the board tended to lean toward stuffy rather than hip and trendy, they'd come up with a plan of attack that combined traditional litigation strategy with innovative ideas that Campbell hoped would please the lot. "You're right. We do have this. Let's go be brilliant."

The Leaderboard campus was hipster deluxe. On their way from the parking lot to the front door, they passed a food truck serving third wave coffee and artisanal donuts. A small crowd of twenty somethings hung out by the truck waiting on their orders. Campbell stood in place and stared at the truck. She remembered reading something about it during their night of research, but whatever it was had gotten lost in the jumble of ideas she'd assembled for the pitch. "Hang on a second," Campbell said to Abby and Grace who were a few steps ahead. When they turned back, she pointed at the truck. "Donut?"

Abby stepped toward her and waved a hand in front of her face. "Deny your nature and look away from the donuts, dear one. After we're done with the meeting, I'll buy you all the donuts you want." She rejoined Grace, and they started to walk toward the building.

"Wait," Campbell said. She knew they would think she was crazy, but her gut told her to go with it. "I have an idea." Before they could protest, she walked over to the truck, happy to see there was only one person in line ahead of her. She watched carefully as dreadlocks surfer dude asked a bunch of questions about the recipes and the cooking method, and then selected both a bacon crusted Long John and a vegan apple fritter.

The woman running the operation asked, "Separate bags?" to which surfer dude smiled and nodded.

Campbell had a million questions. Was this truck here every day? Did surfer dude always get the same thing, and why the strange mix? Maybe he was buying the bacon one for a carnivorous chick for whom he had an unrelenting office crush. Or maybe he just liked an occasional taste of bacon with his plant-based breakfast. But more importantly, Campbell smelled fresh-made donuts, and donuts represented all that was good in the world.

"Looking for something sweet or savory?"

Campbell reined in her thoughts and looked up at the woman who looked slightly familiar. She stared for a moment, and although she couldn't place where she might know her from, she did observe that she was surprisingly trim for someone who was surrounded by donuts on the daily. "I'd like a little of everything, please. Say, two dozen."

Donut lady pointed a pair of tongs at her and grinned. "You look like a woman who likes to try things."

What did that mean? Was donut lady flirting with her? Hell, she was cute and she had a truck full of donuts. For those reasons alone, Campbell was tempted to marry her on the spot. She smiled back at her future wife. "I've been told I'm adventurous."

Donut lady started boxing up various donuts, taking her time to select each one before she placed it in the box. Campbell glanced over her shoulder to see Grace and Abby standing behind her, looking impatient. Donut lady paused. "Are they with you?"

"We're here to perform an intervention," Grace said. "Campbell, remember the time donuts almost caused you to fail your CivPro exam?"

Campbell hung her head in mock embarrassment. "I do." She looked up at donut lady. "I allowed a donut to almost ruin my future. I stopped for donuts on the way to our exam." She motioned to Grace and Abby. "I did it for them, but instead of appreciating my good deed, they scolded me for almost being late for the test. *Almost*," she added pointedly.

"Oh sure, blame us," Abby said. "I hate to break it to you, but as much as I'd love one of those chocolate cake rings of wonder, we're actually going to be late if we don't get moving."

In perfect timing, donut lady handed over the box, holding on for an extra few seconds before she released it to Campbell's grasp and handed her a glazed donut nestled in wax paper. "For you. Pay me on your way out and I'll give your friends here a couple of the chocolate cakes. I'd like your visit to be a good memory and not the tragic donut incident of the year."

"Deal. Wish us luck," Campbell said, knowing her request was silly since donut lady probably didn't have a clue why they were even there. Still, it made her feel good to ask. And she felt good about being here. For good measure, she took a bite of the gratis donut and moaned as the glaze and yeasty goodness melted on her tongue. She had her best friends by her side and a plan of attack that included a box of donut glory. What could go wrong?

They'd barely made it into the lobby before Campbell's rhetorical question got a real life answer. Jerry Stoltz was pacing in front of the reception desk looking like a bull in search of a matador to gore. Campbell handed the donuts to Grace and dodged Jerry's moving form to get to the young receptionist who was somehow ignoring Stoltz's antics. She spotted a large coffee cup from the donut truck on the desk with the word Prairie scrawled where the name would go and took a chance. "Good morning, Prairie. I'm Campbell Clark, here to see Mr. Keith."

No sooner was the word Keith out of her mouth before Jerry came to an abrupt halt inches away from her.

"He's busy."

Campbell inched forward, closing the already tight space between them, but instead of moving back like she'd hoped, Stoltz stood his ground. "I have an appointment," she said.

"So do I," he growled.

Campbell's mind started spinning with possibilities. Was it possible Braxton had scheduled a meeting with his current counsel and the firm he was considering to take over at the same time? Were they supposed to fight to the death in a lawyer's version of the Hunger Games? She wanted to ask Stoltz what he was doing here, but decided it was better to act as if she was nonplussed in order to demonstrate confidence.

The receptionist was looking between them with a mildly curious expression, like she was going to wait until they'd worked things out between them, but when it became clear there was a standoff, she picked up the phone. "I'll let Brax know you're all here."

Satisfied she'd at least accomplished a truce, Campbell turned to join her friends, but stopped in her tracks when she spotted Wynne Garrity approaching from the other side of the lobby. When Wynne noticed her, she froze in place, and Campbell debated ignoring the sighting or facing it head on. She knew from her post reunion snooping that Wynne worked for the same firm as Stoltz, so chances were good she was here with him. With a glance at Abby and Grace, she walked up to Wynne to acknowledge their new status as rivals. "Hello again."

"Hello." Wynne looked her up and down and nodded. "Guess you recovered from your reunion night fun."

Campbell hid a frown and injected her voice with what she hoped was a bright and cheerful tone. "Fun is not something you recover from. It's something you embrace." She jerked her chin at Jerry Stoltz who was pacing in front of the receptionist as if he could conjure Braxton with a high step count. "But I'm guessing if you work for that guy, fun is a foreign concept."

A shadow passed across Wynne's face, and Campbell felt a twinge of regret for the sucker punch. It wasn't that long ago that she'd worked for a hard-assed, irritable, unable to be pleased law partner. If it wasn't for Abby and Grace agreeing to her crazy idea, she might still be under his thumb, staving off her frustration with the promise of a partnership.

"Brax will see you all now," the receptionist said, her voice shaking Campbell out of her musings. There was no time for sympathy. It was game time, and she was ready. If Clark, Keane, and Maldonado, didn't land a big case soon, she might be back in Wynne's position, having to grovel for crumbs in hope of someday earning the big prize.

"See you inside," she said to Wynne, resisting the urge to say "good luck" before turning back toward Abby and Grace. If there was any luck to be had today, she hoped it would be squarely on her side.

❖

Holy shit. Wynne barely registered the receptionist's words as she scrambled to process why Campbell Clark and her pals were standing in front of her holding a giant pink box. Wynne had excused herself to the ladies' room when they arrived at Leaderboard, and she'd only been gone a few minutes, but apparently in that span of time, Campbell Clark and her entourage had sprung up like weeds in the garden of her big case.

Her instinct had been right after all. Campbell was after Braxton's business and there'd been nothing innocent about Campbell running into Braxton at lunch yesterday. How long had this been going on?

"You want to explain that?"

She turned at the sound of Stoltz's whispered growl and feigned innocence. "What?"

Stoltz walked alongside her, keeping his voice low. "Don't what me. Clearly, you know that woman. Who is she and why is she here?"

Wynne took a breath while deciding how to spin the news that they were here for a competition instead of a simple smoothing the client over session. "That was Campbell Clark. She used to work for Hart and Dunn, but she recently struck out on her own. She's here to meet with the board as well."

"How did that happen and why didn't we know about it?"

Wynne wanted to ask if those were rhetorical questions, but she knew she'd only be poking the bear. "I don't know. Campbell and I went to law school together, but other than that, I don't really know her. Braxton didn't mention anything about another firm when I met with him yesterday. Ask Daniel." She motioned to the intern who nodded in agreement. Wynne hated resorting to appealing to Stoltz's ugly habit of giving deference to a man's opinion, but she wanted him off her back to give her time to think. While Stoltz fumed behind her, she followed the receptionist into the boardroom.

Brax was standing at the front of the room, looking like a college kid who'd completely forgotten he had a presentation scheduled, while the other eight board members were seated around the conference table. Wynne surmised by the half empty coffee cups and scattered papers, that the board meeting was already underway. She had never met the Leaderboard directors, but she'd done her homework. With the exception of Logan Rampart, one of Braxton's pals who'd worked with him when Leaderboard was run out of Brax's apartment, all of them had been appointed by Braxton's father who held the purse strings that had seeded Brax's big dreams. She'd read a few articles about how Brax chafed against the restraints of the board, but on the cusp of going public, he didn't want to risk making future stockholders uneasy by creating a lot of upheaval. Which was probably why he was chafing against his lawyers instead.

And there were a lot of lawyers in the room. In addition to her, Stoltz, Campbell, and her law partners, there were two first years Stoltz had insisted on bringing along despite her gentle warning that when it came to lawyers and Braxton less was more.

She'd run into Abby and Grace a few times at various functions, but she doubted either one of them remembered her. Like Campbell, they were social and she was not. She wondered if it was their superior social skills that had appealed to Brax. She knew she had to work on the fact that she was all business when it came to meeting with clients, eschewing small talk as a waste of time for her and them. In her view, she was offering them expedient and economical service, but her annual evaluations all pointed to the fact that she hadn't used her allotted networking funds, and mingling with clients was just as important as getting them a good result. Unspoken was the fact that the faster she closed out a case, the less money the firm made. Seth called networking the people tax, and he was right. Unlike her though he embraced the ability to take clients out for a nice steak dinner, followed by an evening spent in the firm box at a sporting event at one of the local arenas or stadiums, all on the firm's tab. She'd rather be stabbed in the eye than spend what little free time she had with the people she worked for, so she had to make up for her lack of desire to schmooze by being the best at her job. Being the best today meant making sure Stoltz was prepared for whatever questions the board might ask, and she'd done her part, staying up half the night to prepare a lengthy dossier she hoped he'd read.

"I'm going to be perfectly honest," Braxton said. "I have concerns about Rhea Hendricks's lawsuit, not because it has merit, but because of the bad publicity, and I want to be able to trust that the law firm that represents us can handle the litigation both inside and outside the courtroom."

Wynne could feel Stoltz bristle beside her, and she knew from experience that any moment he might leap out of his chair and launch into self-serving oratory. What she wanted to do was reach over, pat him on the head, and say, "I got this," but she also wanted to keep her job, so she fixed her expression into what she hoped looked like genuine concern.

"I'm considering a change," Brax said to the board. "And I've invited the partners of Clark, Keane, and Maldonado to the meeting to give us some contrast. Each firm will have fifteen minutes to present their best case for why we should select them to defend this lawsuit."

An older gentleman seated near the head of the table that Wynne pegged as Artie Fairbanks, the oldest board member, cleared his throat and said, "This seems like a waste of time. Don't we already have a top tier law firm on retainer?" He pointed at Stoltz who sat up straighter in his seat. "Do you have a specific reason for thinking they can't handle the job?"

Wynne watched as Stoltz, unable to resist an opportunity to showboat, sprang from his seat. "We can absolutely handle whatever you need in the way of legal representation." Stoltz turned to Braxton. "You have concerns about how this litigation will affect Leaderboard in the court of public opinion." He thumped his chest. "I get that, and speaking of top tier, we have a public relations firm on retainer that can assist with getting your side of the story, front and center."

"And how would you characterize our 'side of the story'?" Braxton asked. "By the way, your fifteen minutes starts now."

Stoltz strode to the head of the table and very nearly edged Braxton out. "Leaderboard is the gem in the crown of social media. It was inevitable that someone would mount an attack to try to topple its popularity, but Leaderboard will not bow to pressure or alter the way it does business. You have an obligation to your users, to your future shareholders, to provide the very best social media platform, and you will not let its integrity be compromised either by being forced to reveal your confidential algorithms or by altering those algorithms to cater to individuals who are not happy with their experience through no fault of yours."

Wynne kept her face impassive during Stoltz's speech, but inwardly she winced at the way too vague description. Stoltz was probably proud of himself for using the word algorithm twice, correctly, but she doubted he had a clue how Leaderboard actually worked and apparently didn't care enough to learn. To him, all cases were the same and he knew better than his clients, assuming that what they really needed was to be listened to, but never heeded.

"What's the most popular feature of Leaderboard?"

Braxton's question dropped like a pebble in the pond, and the ripples of silence were painful to watch. Stoltz repeated the question back to him like a kid stalling for time, but then nothing. Wynne watched as long as she could stand it, but she could not sit idly by and watch her chance at partnership fizzle away because Stoltz had been too proud or apathetic to read the material she'd prepared for him.

She stood and said, "It's the anonymity of the background program that calculates the results. No one knows exactly how it works, so it's not possible to game the system. Your users, sorry, leaders, do their part by making connections, but the exact formula is top secret. While users would love to be able to crack the code, there's value in having a level playing field, the theory being that anyone can rise to the top of the Leaderboard, not just those who are already popular or well connected. I suppose the allure is similar to telling kindergarteners anyone can be president of the United States. Not entirely true, and unlikely for most, but the idea that you can rise to the top, no matter what your situation, is the embodiment of the American dream."

She finished talking and looked around the room to see everyone's eyes on her, reflecting various reactions. Stoltz looked like he wanted to throttle her, Braxton was grinning, and the rest of the board were a mixture of approval and confusion, but it was Campbell's reaction that caught her attention. She looked surprised, like she hadn't thought Wynne had it in her to distill down the essence of Leaderboard, and Wynne was both annoyed at being underestimated and excited she'd drawn Campbell's attention. Well, Campbell better think again if she thought they were going to give up this client without a fight. Wynne soaked up her moment in the spotlight, surprised to find she didn't hate it.

"Exactly," Braxton exclaimed, fist pumping the air. "Everyone can rise to the top."

Wynne resisted pointing out the irony of his statement considering she was currently in a fight to be at the top of Leaderboard's business and only one firm could win. She looked over at Stoltz who shook his head and motioned for her to keep going, and she spent the balance of her fifteen minutes outlining all the strengths their law firm brought to the table. While she talked, she couldn't help but notice Campbell looked like she didn't have a care in the world. God, how she wished she could feel the same way.

CHAPTER SEVEN

Campbell waited until Wynne took her seat before walking to the front of the room. Wynne had done a good job of laying out the case for Worth Ingram to stay on board, but her presentation, while moving, was staid and worn. Now she, Grace, and Abby had fifteen minutes to steal this case, and they were going to make the most of it.

"My name is Campbell Clark, and I'm a partner at Clark, Keane, and Maldonado. The other named partners are here with me today, and here's why that's important." She paused and took a moment to lock eyes with each board member. "Whatever work we do for you will be performed by a partner, not an associate. I will take the lead, but you can reach any one of us, any time, to discuss any aspect of the case." She motioned to Braxton's laptop sitting on the table. "Grace has just emailed each of you a firm prospectus along with our standard representation agreement as an encrypted file. I can assure you our rates are competitive, and we bring to the table all the experience of a big law firm business and litigation practice, but in a customizable package that we will tailor just for you.

"But enough about the logistics. Right now you'd like to see our strategic plan for winning this case." She paused. None of them had expected that the team from Worth Ingram would be sitting in the room when they made their pitch, and she hesitated to be too specific in case Stoltz decided to co-op their plan if the board decided to keep them on. But vague promises weren't going to sway this board and neither was the hour-long presentation she'd prepared to present. She would have to get to the point fast with hard-hitting specifics. Campbell took a deep breath, opened her Powerpoint, and plunged in.

"Rhea Hendricks is a rising star whose last two singles debuted in the top five on Billboard's country music chart." Campbell pointed at the screen which displayed a trajectory on the right side and a constellation of connections on the left. "She has been in a steady climb on the charts, and until recently, her connections on Leaderboard were consistently increasing in both volume and quality. Her connection rate zoomed to ninety-five percent, in large part due to connections she'd made with some major players in the music industry." Campbell clicked her remote to bring up the next slide. "But she took a tumble in the rankings several months ago, and she's alleging that as a result, she lost a major film role, costing her millions of dollars in income.

"As you know," she said, knowing they probably had no idea, "news broke several months ago about her breakup with fiancé, Dash Wilder. Dash is a superstar in the country music world and his fans are extremely loyal." She clicked to the next slide, which contained a graph. "There is a clear correlation between her breakup and her declining Leaderboard status due to the fact that she lost many of the connections she'd made by virtue of her relationship with Dash.

"By now you probably think I'm more of a gossip columnist than a lawyer." She grinned. "It's true, I do keep up with current events, even those that some of you might find silly, but if your lawyers don't understand your primary product, including its practical applications, then you aren't getting your money's worth. You don't want to have to disclose any information about Leaderboard's proprietary algorithm, but that's exactly what Rhea Hendricks's attorneys will try to get you to do. Our strategy will be to point out all the ways that Rhea Hendricks's own actions killed her star quality and demonstrate that Leaderboard merely reflects the facts, but doesn't make them up. You need our expertise both as lawyers and people who use and understand how social media works to win this case."

She reached behind her and opened the box of donuts. "This morning when we arrived, I spotted a food truck outside the building selling donuts. There was a crowd waiting in line, and I don't know about you, but when I see a crowd outside of a food joint, I figure something good is happening inside." She handed the box to the board member to her right, signaling for him to take one and pass the rest around. "I watched the woman in the truck, the owner and sole donut maker, as she answered questions about the ingredients, the cooking method, everything donut 101, and I was struck by what a completely different experience this was than walking into a big chain donut shop where the kid behind the counter probably doesn't have anything to do with the actual donut making or any input into the process.

"These donuts are amazing because the woman who is selling them put her name right there on the box, and she cares enough about her reputation to stand in that truck and make the donuts herself. Grace, Abby, and I are Clark, Keane, and Maldonado, and we know our way around cases like this one, where your business is being attacked and your reputation is at stake. We will personally handle every aspect of your case, and we stake our own reputation on getting you a favorable result. I'm not sure anything could be as good as these donuts, but we will do our level best to top them."

Campbell shook a few hands as they filed out of the room, noting that Wynne, Stoltz and the rest of the team from Worth Ingram had dashed out of the room the minute she was done. She had a good feeling about the presentation and couldn't wait to talk to Grace and Abby, but before she reached the door, Brax pulled her aside. "Impressive. The donut thing especially."

"Thanks, but that part was easy. I mean, who doesn't like donuts?"

Brax grinned. "No one I want to know." He glanced over his shoulder. "Do you mind sticking around? Grace and Abby too.

We have one more thing to cover in executive session, but then I think we might have some news for you. There's a suite around the corner where you can wait. Prairie will show you."

Campbell stifled the urge to burst into a big grin of her own. "You got it." She walked over to Abby and Grace who were already waiting in the lobby.

"What did he say?"

"They loved it, right?'

"He asked us to stick around. I think that's a good sign. It is, right?"

Grace nodded vigorously. "Definitely. Do we wait here?"

"No, hang on a sec." Campbell walked over to the receptionist. "Hi, Prairie, Mr. Keith asked us to wait. He said there was a suite down the hall."

Prairie looked puzzled for a moment, and then she nodded. "Oh, you mean Brax. Sure, come this way. The rest of the group is already there."

It was Campbell's turn to be puzzled, but she waved to Abby and Grace and followed Prairie down the hall. When they reached the door to the suite, she heard voices coming from the other side, and she instantly knew who "the rest of the group" was. Wynne looked up and met her eyes as she walked into the room, and Campbell spent a moment trying to figure out the emotion she saw reflected back at her. Anger with a touch of envy? In the spirit of healthy competition, Campbell strode over to where Wynne was standing and stuck out her hand. "Good luck."

Wynne stared at Campbell's hand like she viewed the gesture as some kind of trick. Campbell smiled. "Don't worry. I don't bite."

"Good to know." Wynne finally clasped her hand in a firm shake. "You were great in there. You literally had them eating out of your hand."

Campbell laughed. "Donuts, the great persuader."

"I guess."

"Let me guess, you're a no carb kind of girl."

"I eat plenty of carbs, but donuts are a gateway drug."

Campbell assumed a serious expression and nodded. "I'm familiar with this phenomenon. After donuts, it's cake, then ice cream. A slippery slope of sweetness."

"Exactly." Wynne patted her stomach. "Next thing you know you're late to work because you can't fit in your clothes."

"You don't strike me as someone who's ever late to work."

"See? Avoiding donuts has its upside."

"I guess. If that's the way you want to look at it," Campbell said, irrationally pleased they'd managed to bond even if they didn't agree about her favorite sweet snack.

"Wynne, can you come here, please?"

Campbell watched Wynne's smile turn sour at the sound of Stoltz's voice. She wanted to tell her to ignore him, but she knew how it was when the partner said jump. You jumped. Grateful she didn't have to be in that position anymore, she said, "You were great too. No matter what that guy says. Too bad only one of us gets the case."

Wynne looked like there was something she wanted to say in response, but Stoltz called out again, so she simply murmured, "Thank you," and walked to the other side of the room. Campbell watched her go, wondering why she'd never noticed how long her legs were or…

"Making friends with the enemy?"

Campbell tore her attention away from Wynne's backside to find Abby looking at her with a knowing smile. "What?"

"I saw the way you were looking at her."

"Not even."

"Well, she sure has changed since school. She looks great."

"I guess. She seems pretty smart too. Gave us a run for it in there, but I think we have this locked down." She heard the door to the suite open and watched Brax enter the room. "It's go time." Abby and Grace crowded close, and everything in the room came to a halt as Brax clapped his hands.

"Thanks to all of you for showing up on short notice." He cleared his throat. "As you know, since we decided to go public, the board has taken an active role in big decisions that affect the health and reputation of Leaderboard. I may not always agree with their decisions, but I have to believe they care about the future of the company. Today, they've decided who they would like to represent us in the first litigation we're facing. Once we've had a chance to evaluate performance, we can decide who will be best to handle future legal work."

Campbell's head spun as he paused for effect. What did he mean "who will be best to handle future legal work?" Whose performance would he be evaluating? Did this mean they had a shot? By the time she tuned back in, Brax was mid-sentence.

"And you'll work together, but it's important to me that Campbell and Wynne take the lead. Jerry, the board trusts you'll keep a close eye on things." Without waiting for an answer, he finished with a simple "excellent work all around" and left the room.

Campbell turned to Grace and Abby and whispered, "What just happened? I mean I think I know, but I need to be sure."

"We got the case," Abby said. "Congrats, rock star."

"But…"

"We got the case, but we have to work with them," Grace said, pointing to the group from Worth Ingram across the room. "Correction, you have to work with them. He made you and Wynne lead counsel for the defendant aka Leaderboard." She clapped Campbell on the shoulder. "Do us proud, and we might get all of Leaderboard's business."

Campbell stared in the direction Grace had pointed and saw Wynne staring back at her, slowly shaking her head. Stoltz was standing directly behind Wynne, and he didn't even attempt to mask his fury. Without breaking eye contact, he marched over to their group.

"I'm not sure what law school you went to, but at Harvard we learned that it's not okay to poach another attorney's client. Good luck catching up." He stalked off with his entourage in tow, and Campbell watched him go, noting that Wynne stayed behind.

"Looks like we'll be working together," Campbell said.

"If that's what you want to call it." Wynne stood with her hands on her hips. "I get that the client can choose whoever they want, but we've been working with Leaderboard since the beginning, and representing their interests is a little more complicated than conjuring up a bunch of special effects to put in a slide show and serving donuts to the board."

"You're kidding, right?" Campbell said, shaking off Grace's hand on her arm, bucking against the attempt to rein her in. "You know that we all graduated from the same school, so don't act like you are better than we are. I promise you we are more than qualified to handle this case and the rest of Leaderboard's business without your help." She lowered her voice to a whisper and added, "And there are no Jerry Stoltzes at our firm, pretending they do all the work and then taking all the credit when things go well in spite of them."

Wynne's eyes narrowed, but she didn't say anything. Campbell wasn't certain if she was unsure how to respond or merely taking her time to find the perfect zinger, but Wynne's phone buzzed, breaking the spell. Wynne glanced at the screen and then shoved it in her bag.

"Monday. My office. Eleven o'clock. We'll go over the work we've done on the case so far. My secretary will call yours to confirm." Wynne tossed the last few words over her shoulder as she strode out of the room, leaving Campbell staring after those legs again.

"If she's the enemy, you're going to have to stop staring at her like that," Grace said.

"Not staring. I swear."

"Liar," Abby said. "That was your last one. After today, we're only friendly enough to get through this case. Then we go in for the kill."

Suddenly cognizant of the fact they were still standing in their new client's offices, Campbell shook off the confusion of her encounter with Wynne. "Let's get to work."

❖

Wynne paced her tiny office, waiting for inspiration, waiting for a way out of this untenable arrangement, and waiting for—

"Garrity, get out here."

Stoltz to explode. And there it was. Making a mental note to call Seth to debrief once Stoltz was done with her, she stuck her head out the door, but Stoltz wasn't in sight. She spotted Jennifer walking toward her desk with a mug in her hand. "Is he in his office?"

"Yes. Tread lightly."

Wynne nodded her thanks for the unnecessary warning. Stoltz had left the meeting this morning in his own car, and she hadn't seen him since, but she'd been dreading his wrath all afternoon. All she'd wanted to do was go to the nearest bakery and buy a dozen doughnuts. Damn Campbell Clark and her impossible metabolism.

She paused in front of Stoltz's partially open door, and he barked for her to come in before she could knock. He was spooky like that. He was a lot of things she didn't like, but he was also a hurdle she had to jump if she wanted to become partner, and she wasn't about to let a jerk like Stoltz shut her out.

"Have a seat," he said, his voice much calmer than she had expected.

She sat on the edge of the seat, ready to spring into action, and waited for him to start railing about everything that had gone wrong that morning.

"I think we have a good opportunity to use this situation to show Braxton and the board that we are the clear choice."

Wynne resisted the urge to stand up and look behind Stoltz to see if he was being operated by another power. "Okay," she said tentatively.

"Tell me everything you know about Campbell Clark."

The question caught her off guard. "Campbell?"

"Yes, Campbell. The woman who's trying to steal our client." He waved his hand to signal his impatience. "I saw you chatting with her. How do you know her?"

"I don't. Not really. I mean we graduated in the same class at UT, but that's about it. We didn't run in the same circles, and today's the first time we've spoken more than a couple of sentences to each other." She conveniently left out that she'd run into Campbell a couple of months ago at the reunion.

"Well, that's going to have to change. Neutralizing her is the key to keeping Leaderboard's business. Obviously, you'll need to share some things with her so it looks like we're working together, but we'll have to work on a separate strategy to win this case. One that we can whip out at exactly the right moment to show Braxton we are the superior firm."

Wynne wanted to shudder at the idea of Stoltz whipping anything out, but she forced a smile instead. "And I suppose you have some specific idea for how you'd like me to proceed?"

"Yes. First off, schedule your meetings with her at her office, not ours. That way we can control what she sees. We've already done a lot of preliminary work on the case, and she shouldn't benefit from it."

Wynne made a mental note to have Jennifer call Campbell's office and change the location of tomorrow's meeting. "And second?"

"Since you're going to be there anyway, get whatever information you have on their operation. Word is they've barely set up shop, and I doubt they have three clients between them, which probably means they don't have much in the way of support staff. There's lean and then there's too lean to handle a client like Leaderboard. These girls are in over their heads, and it's up to us to protect Braxton from making a big mistake just because he likes to root for the underdog."

Wynne wanted to argue with him, wanted to point out that he was being misogynistic for referring to Campbell and her friends dismissively as "girls," point out that it was inappropriate and unethical to snoop around a rival's office, but she knew her arguments wouldn't have any influence on him and would only make her seem weak in his eyes. Attorneys who wanted to become partner were scrappy, and sometimes scrappy meant taking risks, so she merely said, "Okay. I'm meeting with her Monday."

"Excellent. That's it then."

Wynne stood and started walking toward the door, eager to put some distance between them, but he called out again before she made it across the threshold.

"Wynne?"

"Yes?"

"You do a good job on this little project and that partnership is yours for sure."

She paused for a moment, unsure of the best response to give to someone who was basically telling her to fight to the death. "Thanks. I got this."

Seth was in her office when she returned, sitting behind her desk with his feet propped on the desk. "You look cozy," she said.

"I'm sitting here so you won't. Drinks. Roosevelt Room. Now."

"I can't. I have to work."

"We all have to work, but we also have to play every now and then. Besides, the patent associates are buying. They're celebrating some new engineering coup that I pretended to understand. I helped with some of the transactional work, and they invited me and I'm inviting you. All you have to do is nod your head and act like what they accomplished is the best thing ever."

She hesitated. She could use some Seth time to debrief after everything that had happened today. "Okay, but only for a little while, and only if it's not too loud. I need to talk to you."

"Deal." He lowered his legs from her desk and stood. "Meet you downstairs in five."

She met Seth in the lobby of the building and suggested they walk. "There's no parking down there, and who knows how long this spring-like weather will last." The truth was she figured the stroll would give them more time to talk before they were immersed in a crowd. They were a few steps away from the firm when she blurted out, "Campbell Clark is the bane of my existence."

"Bane? That's a pretty strong word. Sounds like something you need a wizard to help you sort out."

"Okay, she's not an epic bane, but she's definitely a burr under my saddle," Wynne replied, instantly regretting the reference. "You know what I mean."

"Do you want to spend the entire walk talking about what to call this or do you want to tell me facts, woman? Out with it."

"She and her fledging law firm have been hired to represent Leaderboard."

Seth came to an abrupt stop. "Wait, what?"

"You heard me."

"You got fired from the case?"

Wynne shook her head. "I almost wish that had happened. No, we have to work together. At least on the Hendricks case. Once that's over, Braxton implied they would pick one of us to handle their future business."

Seth waved his hand. "Oh, please, there's no way he's ditching Worth Ingram for a start-up."

"A week ago, I would have said there's no way he would even hear their pitch, but he's on a tear about having representation that more accurately reflects his corporate culture—hip and trendy. Everything that Worth Ingram is not."

"Makes sense in a way."

She punched him in the arm. "Whose side are you on?"

"Yours, of course. Look, you just have to get him to see that just because his company is hip and trendy doesn't mean his law firm has to be. He needs lawyers who can deal with the gravitas of the courtroom and who bring venerable veteran force to the table in order to intimidate litigants." He raised his fist. "Might and power, that's what Worth Ingram, with you leading the charge, represent. Campbell Clark and her pals are all lipstick and kisses. You got this."

"I guess so." She appreciated his encouragement, but now all she could think about was the pretty coral shade of Campbell's lipstick and what it would be like to kiss her full lips.

"Wynne?"

She shook away her dreamy thoughts. "Yes?"

Seth pointed at the sign to the Roosevelt Room. "We're here. Are you good?"

She wasn't, but she didn't think talking about it anymore was going to help the situation. Seth had given her what he promised—a pep talk. Now she needed to make it work. "Sure."

An hour later, she nursed a drink at the bar while Seth cruised an associate from the tax section and the rowdy patent lawyers cheered on a pool tournament like it was a Manchester United match. Good thing she'd talked to Seth on the way over because there was no chance they'd be able to have a conversation here. She didn't begrudge him his fun. She'd gotten what she needed and she was ready to do battle to keep Leaderboard's business. Campbell Clark and her pals were going down.

"Is this seat taken?"

Wynne looked up to see a woman leaning on the barstool next to hers. The woman had perfectly coiffed waves of jet-black hair, and she was dressed in a red suit that hugged all her curves. And there were curves for days. Suddenly aware that she'd let her stare travel the entire length of the woman's body, she looked at her face—which was perfect in every way—and realized she looked vaguely familiar. "Uh, yes. I mean, no. No one's sitting here."

The woman slid onto the stool and stuck out her hand. "Lane Jennings. Patents."

That's where she'd seen her, a lawyer at the firm, although Lane didn't fit the usual profile of the patent section posse. Wynne raised her glass. "Ah, you're the one responsible for the free drinks tonight."

"One of the ones." Lane pointed at Wynne's near empty glass. "Can I get you another?"

Wynne considered for a moment. She'd been nursing the same martini since she arrived, regretting her decision to accompany Seth to the bar. It was too noisy and too full of coworkers to have a decent conversation, and she didn't have the luxury of getting drunk because she would have to get some work done when she got home. Still, Lane was nice to look at and everyone in the patent section was a brainiac, so conversation was bound to be stimulating. Her mind flashed to Campbell standing at the front of the Leaderboard boardroom, commanding the attention of everyone in the room with her engaging and original presentation. The last thing she needed was another distraction from a cute girl.

"Actually, I was about to head out."

"That's a shame."

Wynne cast about for a response. A minute ago, she'd figured Lane was just being friendly, but now she heard a trace of flirtation in her voice. Or was she imagining it? Her strange and unwelcome attraction to Campbell had her on edge and likely reading more into this encounter than was actually there. She traced the rim of her martini glass and made her decision. "Thanks for the offer, but I really need to go." She stood before she could change her mind.

Lane smiled, a slow, sexy smile. "Another time maybe?"

"Maybe."

CHAPTER EIGHT

Campbell swiped her hand to strike at whatever was blaring in her ear and heard a crash followed by the sound of something skittering across the floor.

"What is happening?" she exclaimed as she rolled over in bed and squinted at the daylight pouring in through her bedroom window that signaled Monday was already rocking along without her. Making a mental note to buy blackout curtains, she crawled out of bed and retrieved her phone, praying the case was as sturdy as the guy at the store had promised. True to his word, the glass screen was intact, and the calendar alert that flashed across it signaled she didn't have time to snooze. "Justin, you owe me big," she muttered.

The truth was, she owed him for the intro to Brax, and he was merely cashing in. The only good thing about defending a traffic ticket for her brother was that the municipal court was close to her house in South Austin. Everything else about the task was bad. For starters, she'd never appeared in city court before where simple traffic tickets and code violations were handled. She was no stranger to speeding tickets, but her packed schedule had never allowed time to fight them. All she really knew about municipal court was she'd be down there, vying for a dismissal from the prosecutor along with a bunch of random citizens, most of whom were representing themselves, which is exactly what Justin would be doing if he hadn't connected her with Braxton Keith.

She showered and wandered to the kitchen, hoping there was enough coffee left in the house to make a cup for the road. There wasn't. Campbell stood in front of the open cabinet for way longer than necessary to confirm this fact as she tried to remember the last time she'd ordered groceries. Finally, she shut the cabinet door and scratched out a list, vowing that sometime today she would find time to order enough food to make her look like she actually lived in this house.

The house had been her grandparents' place. It was one of the few in the South Congress neighborhood that had stayed in a family rather than being sold off to the highest bidder when the tax rates started to skyrocket. It had been sad to see all the neighbors move out and be replaced by a random mix of hipsters and out of state transplants who didn't balk at the exorbitant real estate prices because they were still more affordable than New York or California, but she was thankful the new residents seemed vested in keeping the houses authentic, rather than mowing them down and replacing them with multistory monstrosities.

The courthouse parking lot was crammed, and the line to get through security was full of clueless people who had pockets full of stuff that set off the metal detectors. By the time Campbell slipped into the courtroom, she'd rehearsed her arguments about how the hidden placement of the speed limit sign was the real culprit involved in Justin's speeding violation as if she was pitching a case to the Supreme Court. She strode confidently toward the bailiff and asked where she could find the prosecutor. He pointed at a harried young man, likely a brand-new graduate from law school, sitting at one of the counsel tables, surrounded by stacks of files. Campbell put on her best winning smile and approached with an outstretched hand. "Good morning, I'm Campbell Clark here on behalf of my client, Michael Justin Clark. I was hoping that we could—"

"Dismissed." He handed her a piece of paper. "Get the judge to sign it."

Campbell stared at the piece of paper until he shook it at her. She pulled it toward her and skimmed the three-line motion to dismiss. "Why?"

He stopped what he was doing and looked at her with a curious stare. "Officer can't make it. I could ask for a reset, but the judge hates it when the officers don't show, and…" he paused and pointed at the stacks of files, "it's not like I don't have anything else to do."

She nodded, gripped the paper, and walked over to the bailiff. She didn't have to say anything. He plucked it from her hand and handed it to the clerk who stamped it with the judge's signature and told her she was all done. She got a copy of the dismissal from the clerk and hightailed it out of the building before anyone could change their minds. It was still early and she had nowhere to be before her meeting at Wynne's downtown office at eleven. Justin's office was close to Wynne's, and she snagged some pan dulce from La Mexicana Bakery and drove downtown. Parking in downtown Austin was one more thing she didn't miss about her old job, but this way she could accomplish two important tasks.

Justin came up to the front desk to meet her a few moments after the receptionist told him she was there. "Did you forget to go to court? Are you here to beg my forgiveness and pledge your eternal service to me?"

Campbell smacked him in the stomach with the bakery box. "Hardly." She pointed at the paper she'd placed on top. "Case freaking dismissed."

He took the paper in both hands. "You're kidding!" He set it and the box down and spun her around. "All those years of arguing with me over the remote have really paid off. You're the best."

She felt a pang of guilt. "Give me a sweet bread, and I'll tell you how it went down."

He opened the box with a flourish and gazed inside while Campbell looked on—so many incredible choices. She settled on a fruit bar pastry, because fruit was healthy, right?

"Okay, dish," he said between bites of his concha.

"Truth? The officer was on vacation, and they're too backed up to reset your case. Total time in court, twenty seconds, tops."

"That's it? I think you still owe me a favor."

"Nope. A deal's a deal. Besides, it's not like your favor to me has actually panned out. Brax hired us to work with his current firm for one case. If the case goes south, he may fire us all, and then I'll be handling everyone's traffic tickets while I find another big fish."

"Damn, I thought the gig with Brax would be a lock. Isn't the other firm a bunch of dinosaurs? I'm surprised he decided to keep them around."

Campbell conjured up a vision of Wynne, the very opposite of dinosaur. She started to mention her to Justin but stopped. She wasn't sure why. "Not sure he had anything to do with that decision. More like his board took over when they saw he was trying to fire venerable and stuffy and replace them with Charlie's Angels."

"Charlie's Angels? Is that what you're calling yourselves?"

"Law school nickname. Not one we gave ourselves. It is catchy, but since there's no Charlie, not really appropriate. We're more like the law firm equivalent of the Ghostbusters."

"Well, whoever you are, I'm sure you're more Brax's speed than a bunch of old guys stuck in the past."

Again with the old reference. Now. Now was the time to mention that not all the lawyers at Worth Ingram were past their prime or guys, and one in particular might even be date-worthy, but her phone chimed to signal it was time to head to Wynne's office. "Speaking of the other law firm, I'm supposed to be there for a meeting in just a few. How about we get together Friday after work and I'll catch you up."

"No can do. I've got a gig, but Perry's birthday is coming up," he said, referring to their younger sister. "Give me a call later and we'll make plans."

Campbell left the office feeling slightly guilty. She and Justin didn't keep secrets, but Wynne wasn't a secret, was she? No, she was a business thing. A smoldering, hot business thing that was getting under her skin.

The lobby of Worth Ingram was decorated with oversized antiques and a hideous combination of artwork in gilded frames with no central theme, as if each of the partners had brought a piece of art from home to be displayed in a scattered arrangement of expensive bad taste. She gave her name to the receptionist who asked if she'd like a cup of coffee while she waited. She declined, but after five, then ten minutes passed while she was kept waiting, she was beginning to wish she hadn't. Finally, the receptionist returned with another woman in tow. The new woman extended her hand with a smile, but Campbell could see a trace of apprehension.

"Hi, Ms. Clark. I'm Jennifer, Ms. Garrity's assistant. I'm afraid there's been a misunderstanding. Ms. Garrity is at your office right now, waiting for your meeting."

Campbell looked at her phone to check her calendar, but there had been no change to the schedule on her end. She pulled up her firm email account and saw a message from about an hour ago from the new receptionist Grace had hired, Blue Dawn. She rolled her eyes at the name and opened the message. *Win Geriti called to confirm your meeting.* And that was it. She quickly typed a reply. "And did you confirm? Did you discuss location? Are you dense?"

She stared at the screen for a moment, and then started backspacing until she was back to the first two sentences. She'd had high hopes for this receptionist since they'd gone through a ton of résumés before they found any applications with experience working at a law firm. She made a mental note to talk to Grace about the new hire and drove to her office, frustrated about the confusion, but unable to contain a growing excitement at the prospect of seeing Wynne again.

Wynne watched while the receptionist at Campbell's fledging firm wrote down her name as Win, but she didn't bother to correct the misspelling. Now that she was an adult, she liked having an unusual name but it had been the bane of her existence early on. Today, she'd take Win and accept it as foreshadowing, because she was going to show up Campbell Clark and her Barbie friends when it came to Leaderboard's business.

"Please have a seat and I'll let Miss Clark know you're here."

Wynne took her time walking back to the group of colorful, modern chairs arranged in the lobby and surveyed the den of her rival. The offices were bright and airy with lots of natural light pouring in from the tall windows. As a senior associate, she had a tiny window in her office at Worth Ingram that overlooked the roof of the building next door, but the majority of the firm was shut off from the natural rhythms of sunup and sundown, likely in an effort to fool all the associates into working round the clock.

"Wynne?"

Wynne turned to see Abby Keane standing behind her, a curious expression on her face. "Hi, I hope you don't mind. I was just admiring your new office while I waited."

"No worries," said Abby. "But do you mind if I ask what you're waiting for?"

These women needed to get their act together. Or not. Wynne glanced at her watch. "I have a meeting with Campbell. Matter of fact, it was supposed to start fifteen minutes ago." Okay, maybe she shouldn't have thrown in that last bit of snideness, but they were both on the clock here, and if Campbell was going to keep her waiting, she'd be better off going back to her office and getting some work done there.

"I know," Abby said. "I mean I know about the meeting, but it's supposed to be at your office, not here. Campbell was going straight there after court this morning."

Wynne shook her head. "My assistant called yesterday to change the location. She confirmed with someone named..." she paused to look at her phone. "Blue Dawn?" Abby jerked her gaze toward the receptionist and uttered a low growl.

"Ugh, I'm sorry. Have a seat and I'll straighten this out."

Wynne watched as Abby walked over to Blue Dawn who had just broken out a Bento box with some seriously pungent food right there at the front desk. She couldn't quite hear every word of the whispered conversation, but she did catch a few snippets.

I can't believe you didn't tell Campbell the meeting had changed.

There are a lot of calls. I can't be expected to remember everything everyone says.

Put that smelly crap away. Your desk is not a dining room.

When Abby headed back her way, Wynne pretended she hadn't been listening, but Abby didn't get a chance to say anything before Campbell burst through the doors.

"What are you doing here?"

Wynne considered several possible responses to Campbell's barked question. "I think there's been a misunderstanding."

"Yeah, that's what your secretary said. Is there some reason you decided to move the meeting here?"

"Is there some reason you don't want me here?" Wynne retorted. She watched Campbell start to respond, but then look over at Abby and Blue Dawn both of whom were staring in their direction in an ironic payback of her own eavesdropping from a moment ago.

Campbell motioned for her to follow. "Let's take this inside."

Wynne followed Campbell past the reception desk to a conference room. Unlike the conference rooms at Worth Ingram that contained massive wood tables and were lined with shelves full of legal treatises no one used anymore, this one was light and airy like the lobby, and the table was a stunning piece of art. "Gorgeous," she murmured.

"What?"

Wynne pointed. "The table. It's beautiful."

"Thanks. It's a custom piece. The top is from Marble Falls."

Fledging or not, the firm had to be doing okay if they could afford an outlay like this. Although maybe they'd gone into serious debt in their quest to impress Braxton Keith. Either way,

Wynne decided she needed to be careful not to underestimate her competition and focus on how to win this case in a way that showcased Worth Ingram's value to Leaderboard's future success. First step, don't let the enemy know you're out to get them. "I'm sorry about the mix-up over where to meet. It was probably my fault. I called yesterday to ask if we could meet here since we have a bunch of depositions scheduled at the office today."

Campbell's face softened into something close to a smile. "It's okay. Besides, I'm pretty sure you could've told Blue Dawn I was on fire and she'd have waited until today to call the fire department."

"I can't even imagine having to be in charge of hiring my own staff on top of leasing a building, computer equipment, and phones, not to mention ordering a custom conference room table. What made you decide to go out on your own?" The question came out before Wynne could censor it, but she was actually glad she'd asked. She was curious, sure, but as an added bonus, maybe she could expose some weakness.

"This seems like the kind of conversation we should have over lunch." Campbell picked up her bag. "Any food allergies? I'm talking legit allergies, not some fad food sensitivity that's a mask for why you don't eat carbs."

"I told you I eat carbs," Wynne said, instantly wishing she could reel the words back in. What was it about Campbell that made her let down her guard? "But I'd really like to get some work done."

"We're going to talk about the case. Is there some reason we have to do that in an office and not a restaurant? Do the powers that be at Worth Ingram say you have to rack up your billable hours sequestered away from the world?"

Wynne heard the challenge, and she wasn't backing down. "Quit acting like you're the only one who has any freedom here. I can do my work however I see fit." She pointed at the door. "Lead the way, but there better be some righteous carbs wherever we're headed because I'm starving."

A few minutes later, they were seated at Guero's, deep diving into a basket of chips and several different salsas. They placed their orders with the waitress and, determined to show Campbell she was game for anything, Wynne resisted ordering a salad in favor of the taco pastor platter.

"I love this place," Campbell said in between bites of chips.

"Me too, but it's been a while since I've been here."

"Where do you like to go?"

"Shouldn't we talk about the case?"

"There's plenty of time for that. I thought it would be nice to get to know each other a little bit first."

Wynne stopped mid-chip and considered the irony. They'd known of each other for years if you counted back to the time they'd spent in law school, but neither one of them knew much about the other. She'd placed the blame squarely on Campbell, but was that really fair since she'd never even tried to get to know her either? Careful to keep her guard up, she figured it couldn't hurt to share an innocuous fact or two. "I confess that I do watch what I eat most of the time, but I have a weakness for burgers. Cheeseburgers. There's this food truck that shows up on—"

"Hold up. Did you say food truck?"

"Yes." Wynne narrowed her eyes. "Why?"

Campbell shrugged. "I don't know. You don't seem like a food truck kind of person."

"Really? I'm going to pretend that you didn't just say that, but to punish you, I'm not going to tell you the name of the truck." She wagged a finger. "No cheeseburgers for you." The waitress showed up at that moment with their food, and Wynne ignored Campbell's steady gaze by focusing on her food. She'd eat half and have the rest wrapped up for later. "Let's talk about the case."

Campbell looked like she wanted to protest, but she said, "Okay. It doesn't look like you've responded to discovery yet."

"No, we still have a little time, but we do have draft responses ready to go. To be honest, it's been hard getting Braxton to sit down and review the responses."

"Brax."

"What?"

"Brax. You called him Braxton. Maybe if you called him what he wants to be called, he'd be more likely to respond to you."

So this was how it was going to go. Wynne put her fork down, her appetite quickly deteriorating. "You do know that Braxton and I were getting along just fine until recently?"

"I know that he wouldn't have been shopping around for a new attorney if that were the case."

"Look, Braxton and Stoltz have a tendency to butt heads, but that's a personality thing. We have been doing great work for Braxton and Leaderboard, and until you showed up there were no complaints." Wynne didn't care in this moment if she was being entirely accurate, but she carried her logic a step further. "It's not a very auspicious start to your firm to steal clients. What did you promise to get him to bring you on board?"

Campbell set her fork down slowly, but what she really wanted to do was stab Wynne with it. Instead she took a drink of water, then dabbed at her mouth with her napkin while she counted to ten. When she finally felt like she could speak without cursing, she crossed her arms and said, "I didn't poach your client. You don't know me very well, but I'm telling you, that's not my style."

"Okay."

"Okay? That's all you have to say?" Campbell could tell by Wynne's curt tone that it was far from okay.

"What do you want me to say?"

Good question. Campbell wasn't sure she had an answer. "I don't know. Maybe something like, 'You're right, I don't know you very well. Why don't we get to know each other better and maybe it'll be easier to work together.'" Wow, she hadn't expected that overture to come tumbling out, but now that it had, she decided it was brilliant. The best way to win Leaderboard's business was to find out exactly why Braxton was on the outs with them. Alienating Wynne wasn't going to get her any inside info, but cozying up to her might.

"I think I know you pretty well."

Campbell heard the sarcasm behind Wynne's words, but she ignored it in favor of her new master plan. "Not even. We barely saw each other in school, and that was years ago." She stuck out her hand. "Campbell Clark, nice to meet you. I'm working on the Leaderboard case. You know the one. Oh wait, aren't you working on it too? See, we already have something in common."

Her hand hung in the air for an awkward moment until Wynne finally reached out to grasp it. "Wynne Garrity, nice to meet you too."

"We're off to a great start. Now, tell me something fun you like to do and let's make a plan. It'll be our reward for a day of hard work." Campbell watched Wynne's puzzled expression. "Come on, it can't be that hard to think of something you enjoy. Tell me big law hasn't killed all the joy in your life."

"I happen to enjoy working for a big firm."

"Said no one ever."

"Are you trying to start a fight right on the heels of offering to plan a fun outing?"

"Who me? Never. Did you think of something?"

"Why don't you surprise me?"

Campbell studied Wynne's face, certain she'd heard a trace of flirtation, but she couldn't get a read on whether it was intentional. Convinced she'd imagined it, she pressed on. "Okay. Don't make plans for Friday after work. I'll text you the details later."

"This Friday?"

"No time like the present. Why, do you have other plans?"

Wynne shook her head. "No, I just…never mind. Friday's great."

Campbell wanted to ask more about the source of Wynne's hesitation, but she didn't want to upset the balance of the truce they'd struck. "Perfect. Now that we've got that out of the way, let's talk about the pleadings that you've filed so far."

As Wynne outlined what documents had been filed, Campbell asked questions and nodded in response to Wynne's answers, but she found she was more focused on figuring out the perfect outing, away from all the legal mumbo jumbo. She told herself the opportunity to hang with Wynne in a nonprofessional setting would be a great way to soften her up and get her to reveal some inside scoop about Leaderboard that she could use to win their future business, but deep inside she knew she just wanted to spend some personal time with the enigmatic and very attractive Wynne. She'd have to tread very carefully here.

Chapter Nine

Friday afternoon, Wynne surveyed the top of her desk and was pondering lighting fire to the stacks of files cluttering the surface when Seth burst through her door.

"Did she call you?"

Wynne stared at him, trying to figure out how he knew about her date with Campbell. Well, not a date really. An outing. A get to know you better so we can have a better working relationship kind of outing. But one that she wasn't telling anyone about because when she'd practiced that whole spiel out loud it had sounded suspect. She fixed her face into what she hoped was an innocent, or at least neutral expression. "What?"

"Lane, from patents. She asked me for your number. Which is silly really since she can just dial your extension or send you an email, but maybe she doesn't want to ask you out that way. Anyway, I gave her your number today at lunch. Has she called?"

She pointed at the chair in front of her desk. "You, sir, are making no sense." She pulled out her cell and saw she had two unread text messages. The first one was from Campbell, confirming she would pick her up at seven, punctuated with a smiley face. She wasn't a fan of emoticons, but she couldn't help but smile as she read the text. The second was from a number she didn't recognize. She scrolled through the message. *Remember me from the happy hour? I'd love to meet and buy you that drink I owe you. Maybe even dinner if you're up for it. Looking forward to hearing from you, Lane.*

"Well?"

Wynne looked up at Seth who was watching her with an eager expression. "You gave out my cell number? Really?"

"I did. Three reasons." He held up a hand and ticked them off. "She's hot. She's smart. And you need a fling."

"I don't need a fling."

"You do. All work and no play. You know the rest."

"I think the rest is 'she gets a partnership, and then she can play.'"

"Or she turns into a shell of a person. Look, I get it, but you're entitled to have a little bit of you time. Hell, a fling might even relieve some tension and make it easier to get your work done. Did I mention reason number one? She's hot."

"Quit saying fling. I'm not looking for a fling, whatever that means."

"We both know what it means, and you should be. Fun with a hot woman in a way that won't distract you from your work. It's the perfect solution. Go out with her tonight—it's Friday. The universal date night."

At the words "hot woman," Wynne had a flash of Campbell standing in front of the board at Braxton's offices, commanding the attention of everyone in the room. She shook her head to clear the image. "Not going to happen. Besides, I'm busy tonight."

"Yeah, I know. You're working." Seth sighed and stood. "The first step is admitting you have a problem. Look, I want to be partner too, but you've got to find some balance here or you're going to work yourself silly."

"Duly noted. Now scurry on out of here so I can balance this bunch of crap," she said, pointing to the files on her desk, trying to ignore what it meant that she hadn't corrected his assumption that she was working tonight. Well, she was kind of working. Seeing Campbell was work-related, wasn't it? Wynne groaned, wishing she'd never put herself in this position.

She waited until she was certain Seth had left the office suite before gathering her things and heading for the door. Jennifer was at her desk, and Wynne felt instant guilt because she didn't remember a time when she'd left before Jennifer.

"Have something fun planned?" Jennifer asked.

"I'm not entirely sure," Wynne said without thinking. "Actually, I'm meeting Campbell Clark to talk about the Leaderboard case."

"Ah, so a working evening. At least you have someone pleasant to spend it with."

"You know Campbell?"

"She was here looking for you the other day when there was that mix-up about the schedule. She seems nice. Cute too," Jennifer added with a sly smile before shooing her away with one hand while she pointed at Stoltz's door with the other. "You should get out of here quick. If he sees you, you'll never get to leave."

"Are you sure I shouldn't stay?"

"Git."

Wynne walked briskly to the elevator, and a few minutes later, she was standing outside the building. She froze in place, staring at the way the setting sun cast a glow over the sky. Her window in the building faced the east, and she couldn't remember the last time she'd seen the sun set. The view was breathtaking.

"Excuse me."

Wynne glanced around for the source of the voice, but was too late as the man walking by jostled her out of her reverie. She wasn't sure how long she'd stood in the same spot, staring at the sky, but apparently long enough to become a menace to other pedestrians. She fished her keys out of her bag and headed to the parking garage to retrieve her car.

Once she got home, she stood in front of her closet, wondering what to wear. What she really wanted to be doing was curling up on the couch with her laptop, but Campbell would be here in thirty minutes, and Wynne suspected she wouldn't accept a cancellation at the last minute. Her persistence was likely the reason she'd been able to horn in on the Leaderboard case, and Wynne decided to take a page from her book. She could be persistent too, and tonight she planned on doing whatever it took to find out more about Campbell's new firm so she could find and exploit their weaknesses. Maybe she'd get to bill for her time tonight after all. Bonus.

❖

Campbell fired off a text to Wynne to tell her to dress casual, plugged Wynne's address into her phone, and drove the short distance from her house to Wynne's. She'd been surprised that Wynne had suggested they meet there. She seemed so private and closed off. Campbell didn't know any personal details about her, which was kind of weird since they'd spent three years in school together not that long ago. She remembered Wynne had always been the first one to raise her hand in class, but outside the classroom she was a behind the scenes kind of person, working on law review instead of the moot court teams like she and Abby and Grace had done, and studying with just Seth instead of the larger study groups that many of the students favored. Other than knowing Wynne was smart, Campbell didn't know much about her, and she was looking forward to seeing where she lived, hoping it would give her some insight into the woman she had to best to win Leaderboard's business.

The house was small, but it was in the Rainey Street historical district, an area of town that had recently become gentrified causing house prices to skyrocket. Many of the neighbors had put up quirky yard decorations in keeping with the eclectic neighborhood of bungalow style houses, but Wynne's yard and porch were unadorned, with not even a potted plant in sight. Campbell pulled into the driveway, wondering what kind of car was parked in Wynne's garage. Was it a sensible ride with good fuel economy and safety features, or did she have a secret passion for fast cars with sporty features?

Campbell had barely knocked on the door before it flew open. Wynne had a purse in one hand and her keys in the other. She'd dressed causally in jeans, loafers, and a dark blue linen shirt that deepened the blue in her eyes, and Campbell drank in the sight, dumbfounded by the difference between business Wynne and casual, after-work Wynne. She liked this version. A lot.

"Am I dressed appropriately for whatever you have planned?"

Campbell let her gaze linger for a moment before answering. "Absolutely."

Wynne cleared her throat. "Ready to go?"

Campbell cast about for a reason to get inside the house, unable to explain her strong desire to see more of Wynne's personal side. "Aren't you going to invite me in?"

Wynne looked uncomfortable. "I wasn't planning on it. Don't we have some mysterious place to be?"

Campbell considered pressing, but Wynne's brisk demeanor told her if she wanted to get Wynne to open up to her, forcing this issue right now wasn't a smart move. Besides, they didn't have a ton of time to get where they were going. "You're right. Mysterious place coming right up." She jingled her keys to her Audi TT, and a few minutes later, they were speeding along the highway.

"At some point I'm going to realize where we're headed," Wynne said. "Are you sure you don't want to go ahead and tell me?"

"Oh, I'm sure."

"Not even a hint?"

"Not even."

"Fine," Wynne said. "I'll let you try to distract me with idle conversation. How was your day?"

Campbell took her eyes off the road for a moment to look at Wynne, surprised to see genuine curiosity reflected in her eyes. "It was okay. We're in the process of looking for a new receptionist, you'll be glad to know. It's kind of amazing to me how many people apply for a job when they have absolutely no experience."

"I can't imagine having to deal with hiring and firing people in addition to all the other work I have on my plate."

"But when you make partner, you'll start to have some administrative responsibilities. You want to make partner, right? I mean, that's really the only reason to keep working for someone like Stoltz, isn't it?"

"Yes, but it's a big firm, and the administrative stuff is dealt with mostly by the managing partner."

"Which means you get little to no control over your career."

"I have plenty of control."

"Name one decision you can make that you don't have to run by someone else." Campbell shook a finger in Wynne's direction. "Something important, not whether or not to buy a client lunch or invite them to sit in the firm's box seats at a Longhorn game." She turned back to the road, noting the silence that hung in the air between them.

"I thought the purpose of this little outing was to get away from the office, but it seems like you want to pick a fight with me."

Campbell instantly felt bad for pressing the issue. She wasn't sure why it was so important that she convince Wynne the path she'd taken was superior, but clearly she was dumping her own issues on Wynne. She couldn't imagine that Wynne was happy at Worth Ingram, but why did she care? "You're right. I'm sorry. I actually do have something fun in store for tonight, and it's only mildly work related." She pointed to the right at a large crowd standing in line outside the Moody Theater. "We're almost there."

"Where are we?"

"You're kidding, right?" Campbell watched Wynne's face for a smile to signal she was joking, but all she saw was a blank stare. "We're at the Moody. Home of *Austin City Limits*. The show? Is any of this ringing bells for you?"

Wynne nodded slowly. "You know I read an article about this place last month. What are we doing here?"

Campbell smiled broadly. "We're here to see a taping. Rhea Hendricks is playing here tonight."

"You're kidding? Wait, I thought it was a lottery." She pointed. "Look at that crowd. We're never getting in."

"Ah, see you do know something about this place."

"Only what I read. The article said they don't sell tickets to the show—you have to sign up for the lottery a few days in advance." Wynne narrowed her eyes. "Did you sign up this week? Are you really that lucky?"

"Oh, I'm pretty lucky," Campbell said before she winced at the suggestive tone she hadn't intended. "But not that lucky." She pointed at the line. "We are skipping that action." She steered the car to the back of the lot and parked in a space marked Staff.

"Now I'm really confused."

"No need. Just trust me." Campbell watched Wynne's skeptical expression and brushed it off. This chick was a tough cookie. If she was smart, she'd stop trying to win her over, but Campbell's instincts told her she was better off giving the appearance they were forming an alliance. It was a little early in the process to get adversarial, especially when part of this game was to pretend they were working together. Earlier that day, she'd watched a TED Talk that Brax had given last year about the benefits of groupthink. While she didn't think it had been his idea to keep Worth Ingram on the case, she did imagine that her ability to work well with others would be a factor in Leaderboard's decision about who to give their future business. Time to put that idea to the test. She sent a quick text and then shoved her phone in her purse. "Let's go."

Campbell led the way to the back of the building, taking special notice that Wynne stuck really close. Close enough for her to smell the crisp, clean scent of Wynne's perfume. Some kind of citrus. Lemons?

"Are we going in or are we going to stand here and listen from the outside?" Wynne asked, breaking the spell.

Campbell smiled to cover her lack of focus and knocked on the door. Within seconds, it swung wide to reveal her beaming brother on the other side. "About time," he said with a lopsided grin.

"Shut up," she said, playfully punching him in the shoulder. "Say you're glad to see me. Say it."

"Little bit."

They both turned at the sound of a clearing throat to find Wynne staring at them. "Are you going to introduce me?"

Campbell looped her arm through Justin's. "Wynne Garrity, meet my big brother, Justin."

Wynne nodded. "Nice to meet you." She reached out and shook his hand. "You work here?"

"More of a hobby than a job," he said.

"More like an obsession," Campbell said. "Justin was obsessed with Guitar Band when we were growing up, and now he'll do whatever it takes to be part of the music scene, even if it means working the door."

"Hey now," he said. "Who's doing who a favor here?"

"Sorry, bro. Did you manage to snag us seats?"

"When have I ever let you down?"

"You want a list?"

"Are you two always like this?" Wynne asked.

"Like what?" Campbell said at the exact same time as Justin. "Oh, the sparring? Yes, pretty much. Most people get used to it. Do you have siblings?"

Wynne's face clouded over. Campbell instantly knew she'd struck a cord, and she scrambled to ease the tension. "Because if you don't, you're lucky." She pointed at Justin. "This guy tried to steal every girlfriend I've ever had."

The flash of surprise in Wynne's eyes was subtle, but Campbell was certain she'd seen it. Surely Wynne already knew she was gay. It wasn't like she'd had any time to date in law school, but she'd always figured most of the people in their class knew she was a lesbian. The idea that she might have just come out to Wynne standing backstage at ACL made her nervous for some reason. And when she was nervous, she couldn't stop talking. "Not that I've had a ton of girlfriends. I mean, with law school, and work, and then starting a new firm, there hasn't been much time to date, and—" Campbell stopped abruptly, hearing the replay of her ramblings in her head and wishing she could rewind back to never mentioning girlfriends in the first place. She turned to her brother with pleading eyes. "Justin, aren't you going to show us around?"

"Sure, sis," he said with a grin. "I've got a few minutes to spare." This time he looped his arm through Wynne's, addressing her instead of Campbell. "What would you like to see?"

Campbell watched them walk ahead of her, unable to stop staring at Wynne's butt. She blamed the jeans. It had to be the jeans or she would've noticed before exactly how tight and round and—

"Are you going to join us?"

Campbell looked up, straight into Wynne's eyes which were twinkling with mischief. She didn't think she'd ever seen Wynne smiling so broadly, and she enjoyed the shine of her smile. Almost enough to forget the embarrassment of being caught ogling.

Wynne tried to focus on what Justin was saying, but she couldn't stop thinking about Campbell staring at her. Like she was interested. In that way.

Not a chance. It wasn't like she hadn't heard Campbell was a lesbian. Seth had told her he knew it for a fact, but he had a tendency to exaggerate the power of his gaydar, and leaned toward thinking everyone played for their team. But she was taken off guard a little by how easily Campbell mentioned the subject, like sharing deeply personal information was no big deal. She hoped Campbell wasn't expecting reciprocity. To deflect, she turned her attention to Justin. "Show me your favorite thing about this place."

"My favorite thing is the Willie Nelson statue outside, but we don't have time to check that out. This visit, anyway." Justin led the way out to where they could see the stage. "No seat in the theater is more than seventy-five feet from the stage." He pointed toward the ceiling. "Upstairs there's a photo gallery featuring the work of Jim Marshall, the former staff photographer for *Austin*

City Limits. It's the largest collection of his work, and it's pretty amazing."

"Justin thinks anything to do with this place is amazing," Campbell said with a teasing tone. "He's been obsessed with the show since we were kids."

"How did you wind up working here?" Wynne asked, curious about the backstory.

"Lots of patience and a bit of stalking. I volunteered a million years ago, but it took me forever to get a gig, and I'm still just a volunteer."

"A volunteer with backstage passes," Campbell whispered behind her hand. "Although he's kind of stingy about sharing."

"Then I feel special," Wynne said, hoping Campbell didn't read a double meaning into her words. Well, half hoping. Part of her enjoyed the idea of being here with Campbell, away from the office, the stacks of files, and the demanding clients. She could barely remember the last time she'd been on a date. Not that this was a date, but it was as close as she'd been in a very long time. "So, what's the plan?"

"There's a couple of tables set up with food in the back. I'll drop you off and you can mingle with whoever you find back here. Just remember to be super quiet when the show starts since they're filming. The set won't be long, and we can meet up after." He looked at Campbell. "Right?"

"Right."

Campbell swept her hand through the air, motioning for Justin to lead the way, and then she reached back toward Wynne. Wynne stared down at her outstretched hand, scrambling to decide how to react, when Campbell waved her forward. "Let's go."

And just like that, the situation defused and Wynne wondered if she'd imagined that Campbell had been reaching for her hand. Of course, she'd imagined it. The question was, why was her mind even going there? Focus, focus. She breathed deep and smiled. "Lead the way."

Less than an hour later, after grazing through the craft services table and watching the band set up, she and Campbell were perched on a couple of stools in the wings, listening to Rhea Hendricks's sultry country folk ballads. Wynne risked a side glance and watched Campbell sway in time with the ballad as if she were transported to another place. Before she could look away, Campbell turned and smiled like she was pleased to see Wynne watching her.

"You like?" Campbell whispered.

"I do. Not my usual fare, but it's really nice. Very mellow."

Campbell pointed toward the stage. "I love this part."

Wynne listened to Rhea sing a soulful refrain about a forever kind of love, and the way she dug deep into the notes made her believe she was relaying a real life experience. She watched Campbell be transported by the melody, and for a moment, she let herself go along for the ride. The words, the tune, everything about the moment, was magical, and she felt suspended in time, completely free.

The set ended too soon, and when it did Wynne stayed on the stool, unsure what Campbell had planned next. She didn't have to wait long.

"Ready to meet the band?"

"What?"

"The band. Justin said that Rhea has an interview with a reporter from *Texas Monthly* right after the show, but we can have a few minutes with the rest of the band before they go out to meet their fans."

Being backstage was one thing, but Wynne had no desire to kill the magic of the evening with the reality of the people behind it. "I'm not much of a groupie. I think I'll just wait for you."

Campbell laughed. "Groupie? That's cute. Seriously, come with me to talk to them. You never know—they might have some dirt on their lead singer. If nothing else, we might get some leads we can follow up on later."

Wynne's brain started clicking as the spell of the music faded away and she started to grasp what Campbell had in mind. "Wait a minute. You want us to talk to them about the case?"

"Of course, that's why we're here."

"We can't do that."

"What do you mean?"

"I mean, what if they do say something that we can use at trial? Neither one of us can be a witness, so if they get on the stand and change their tune," she winced at the unintended pun, "then we can't contradict them. If you want to interview witnesses, we need to do it the right way, with a private investigator."

"Seriously?" Campbell stood with her hands on her hips, all semblance of the misty-eyed, concertgoer gone. "You're really lecturing me on the rules of civil procedure right now?"

"It kind of seemed like maybe you needed a refresher course."

"Next, you're going to tell me that because you made better grades than I did, you get to call the shots." Campbell wagged a finger. "Not even. I know what I'm doing. Remember, I've been doing this exactly as long as you, and I don't have to answer to someone like Stoltz. I actually run my own shop now."

"You might just run it into the ground if you're not careful." Wynne started to say more, but an exaggerated throat clearing behind her interrupted her spin.

"Uh, ladies, you might want to take it down a notch or you're going to get us kicked out," Justin said, touching a finger to his lips.

Campbell frowned. "Sorry, guess we got a little exuberant. Can we still meet the band?"

"No worries. Come on."

Wynne watched Campbell follow her brother, acting like nothing had happened, while she stood in place, still trying to process their interaction. Nothing was resolved, yet Campbell acted like it was. How did she do that?

As if she could read minds, Campbell looked back over her shoulder. "Are you in?"

Wynne wavered. Clearly, Campbell was going to talk to the band whether she did or not. She could join her or be left behind. What if Campbell discovered something really important to the case and shared it with Braxton, claiming all the glory? She couldn't let that happen. If there was glory to be claimed, she wasn't going to stand by and watch Campbell hog it all. Campbell's words echoed. If she wanted a partnership, which she did, she did have to answer to Stoltz, and she had no doubt what Stoltz would do in this circumstance. Not that she wanted to ever be part of the What Would Stoltz Do club, but maybe she could make an exception to the rules to take advantage of this opportunity. Telling herself it would just be this once, Wynne plastered a big fat fake smile on her face. "Oh, I'm definitely in."

CHAPTER TEN

Monday morning, Campbell carried three cups of mocha java into the office conference room to meet with Abby and Grace. She'd made the coffee with the new machine she'd purchased over the weekend. She'd told herself the new coffee maker was to help her cope with Monday mornings, but in truth her bout of retail therapy had been to cope with an entirely different problem, and that problem's name was Wynne Garrity. Despite her best efforts, she hadn't been able to get Wynne out of her head. Not lawyer Wynne, but sexy, cute butt in denim Wynne. It was time for a meeting with her peeps to sort things out.

"Okay, everyone. I've called you here for two reasons, the first of which is to try this amazingness." Campbell set two of the cups down and raised hers to her mouth, taking a moment to let the velvety foam caress her lips. "Delicious," she murmured. She pointed to Grace's cup which was still sitting on the conference room table where she'd placed it. "Aren't you going to try it?"

"Oh, I'm sure it's delicious."

"Then drink up, woman. Or are you mad at me for spending the money on the espresso machine? Because I'm telling you if you are, your anger is misplaced. Clients will flock to our offices to partake of this java wonder. Trust me. A cup of this and one of those donuts from that amazing food truck outside Leaderboard, and we'll have them eating out of our hands."

"Literally," Abby said. "Make a note. If the law gig doesn't work out, we can open a coffee shop, but count me out as the one to get up early to make the donuts." Her aversion to early mornings was well known to all of them.

Grace shook her head. "How could I be mad about a nice Sumatra? It's like you don't know me." She took a sip and sighed. "That's wonderful. But you know what's not wonderful?" She barely waited two beats before launching in. "Madge quit."

"Who's Madge?" Campbell asked.

"Uh, the receptionist. Not the one that mixed up your meeting with Wynne, but the one after that. You know, the one I hoped would be the last one I had to hire because unlike the others, she wasn't crazy. At least not in an obvious way."

"Was she the one with the beehive hairdo?" Abby asked.

Grace glared in response, and Campbell said, "It's official. I'm going to stop learning their names until they stick around for at least a month. Why did she quit?"

"She had her palm read over the weekend and her lifeline said that she was going to meet the love of her life at the beach."

Campbell waited for Grace to start laughing, or do something to show she was kidding, but she got nothing. "Hold up. I thought you said she wasn't crazy."

"Crazy is relative when it comes to hiring receptionists, apparently."

"Okay," Abby said. "But I'm still not getting why she abandoned us."

"She's moving to Galveston to broaden her prospects," Grace said.

"Well, that makes perfect sense," Campbell replied.

"Focus, people," Grace said. "I think we need a different approach to our employee search. The online ads aren't cutting it."

Campbell took another sip of coffee. "What do you suggest?"

"Between the three of us we should be able to come up with some names. If we weren't satisfied working for big firms, surely there has to be support staff who hate it there too."

"That's a great idea," Abby said. "The only people who have it worse than associates are secretaries and paralegals. The senior partner in my section called our secretary when she was on a cruise to ask her where she kept the paper clips."

"I know, I know," Campbell said, "but are you really suggesting we poach someone from our former employers?"

"Not necessarily." Grace steepled her fingers like she did when she was deep in thought. "Didn't you say that Wynne's secretary is super efficient?"

Campbell shifted in her chair at the mention of Wynne's and Grace's uncanny ability to bring up topics that were festering in the back of her brain. "Yeah, no."

"Wait a minute," Abby said. "It's not entirely a bad idea. I mean she probably has a lot of the inside scoop about the Leaderboard case, right? Bringing her on board would be a big coup."

"Stop it." Campbell waved her arms for emphasis. "I'm all about working behind the scenes to steal Worth Ingram's client, but you're not seriously thinking we can just lure their secretary away while we're supposed to be working together?" She watched Grace and Abby exchange knowing smiles. "What's going on?"

"Why don't you tell us?" Abby leaned back in her chair and crossed her arms.

"Tell you what?" Campbell willed away the nervous edge to her voice. There was absolutely no way Abby or Grace would have any idea about her silly attraction to Wynne. Could they?

"I ran into Justin yesterday at Jo's," Abby said, referring to their favorite coffee joint on South Congress. "He mentioned your little rendezvous at ACL with your 'hot lawyer friend.'"

Damn. Campbell scrambled for words. She hadn't bothered to mention the outing to either Grace or Abby. She'd told herself it was because she hadn't learned anything on her trip that was relevant to the case, but the truth was she hadn't wanted to deal with their questions about what exactly she'd been doing with Wynne and why she hadn't asked them to tag along. This looked bad and she knew it. "I have a confession."

"Spill." Grace leaned forward. "No, let me guess. The new espresso machine was a guilt purchase, yes?"

"No. I mean, maybe. Okay, yes." Campbell hung her head.

Abby raised her mug. "Here's to more guilt in the near future." Grace shot her a scowl and Abby shrugged. "Who am I to turn down good coffee? Although next time maybe you can get one of those donut machines where you pour the batter in and then the donuts come out on a little conveyor belt. Clients would love those."

"Who are you kidding?" Campbell said, grateful for the distraction. "Clients would never get to taste them after you finished with them."

Grace cleared her throat. "Are we going to talk about this, and by 'this' I don't mean donuts or espresso."

Campbell stared at them while her feelings tumbled their way through her mind in incoherent strands. Before she could untangle them enough to form a coherent sentence, words started tumbling out. "I like her. I mean she's infuriating, but she's hot too and smart. And smart is hot. Like super smart, but stubborn, which is annoying, but there's something else. Maybe a vulnerability underneath the icy veneer. You know the kind—you just want to melt it, but it's hard because that's not what this is about…" She paused to gauge their reactions and was met with blank stares. "I'm not making any sense, am I?"

"Oh, you're making plenty of sense," Grace said. "You want to get in our competition's pants."

Was it as simple as that? Campbell rolled the thought around in her head, cycling through the possibilities. The idea of getting in Wynne's pants, though she hadn't gone there until just now, was definitely a lure, but it was something else that she couldn't quite articulate. Something that was distracting her from her work, and if she wasn't careful it could get in the way of her relationship with Abby and Grace. She shook her head. "I don't. I mean, maybe I do, but it's not going to happen. I think I just need a distraction. We've all been so busy with work we haven't had time for a personal life, and if we don't have time for a personal life then what was the point of starting this venture?" She watched their faces, hoping they believed her words more than she did.

"You're right," Abby said. "As soon as we get things fully up and running, I plan to take a long vacation to an all-inclusive resort. I'm going to toss my phone in the ocean, plant my butt in a lounge chair on the beach, and sip fruity drinks with little umbrellas in them. What about you, Grace?"

Grace looked back and forth between them as if she wasn't totally buying into the discussion, and Campbell held her breath. Abby knew her pretty well, but she and Grace had been friends since high school, and she didn't have high hopes she'd let her revelation go so easily. She was right.

"Sure, a vacation would be nice," Grace said, "But I can promise you it won't involve messing around with one of our rivals."

Campbell wanted to argue the point that a girl didn't always pick who she was attracted to, but she knew it would only deepen Grace's suspicions. Besides, she wasn't sure she believed her own argument. She *could* choose to ignore her attraction to Wynne, and she had to if she was going to get what she really wanted— Leaderboard's business. She raised her mug. "Let's toast to having a personal life, after this case is over. Now, about that, I need some help." She told them about the trip to ACL and how she and Wynne had talked to Rhea Hendricks's band. "They barely had any dish at all."

"And if they had?" Abby asked.

"I would have gathered intel and reported back." Campbell started to squirm under Abby's piercing stare. "Okay, okay, maybe it wasn't the most well thought out move, but I figured it couldn't hurt to see if they were willing to talk. Wynne wasn't having any of it. Not at first anyway."

Abby nodded. "Your instincts were spot-on, but maybe Wynne had a point." She glanced at Grace who gave her a subtle nod. "I know you're used to busting in with a big plan, but there's just us three to absorb the fallout. Maybe we should talk strategy together before any one of us goes off the rails in the future."

Campbell nodded. She knew Abby was right. She'd been raised to think outside the box, and her creativity was the one thing she could always count on to garner praise, even if it sometimes meant she leaped before she looked. And that was precisely what she was doing with Wynne now that she thought about it. "I promise I'll play by the rules from here on out, and the only goal I have my sights set on is Leaderboard's business."

They finished up their meeting with a lively discussion about how they were going to find a receptionist who didn't suck. Campbell participated like she was completely on board, but in the back of her mind she was working on a plan to get thoughts of Wynne out of her head. It wasn't working.

❖

Wynne looked up to see Stoltz framed in her doorway, and she mentally ran through a list of reasons why he would have come to her instead of summoning her to his office like usual.

"Braxton hired an investigator. You'll meet him tomorrow. He wants you to bring that other chick. See if you can get there early and get the jump on her."

Before she could sort through the string of pronouns, he was gone and Jennifer appeared in his wake. "Sorry about that," Jennifer said. "I tried to warn you he was on his way in, but I got caught on a call."

"It's okay. Do you know anything about this?"

"Not much. Braxton called about it this morning, and he's already arranged for Campbell to be at the meeting."

Campbell. Despite their task of working together, Wynne had managed to avoid seeing Campbell since their weird outing to *Austin City Limits.* Weird wasn't quite the word. She'd actually had fun, and for a few moments had managed to forget that she and Campbell were in competition. But the moment Campbell had dropped her off that night, she'd been plotting her own strategy about the Leaderboard case—a strategy she had no plans to share with Campbell. And now this? "I actually have a couple of phone calls in to investigative firms we've used in the past. Do you think Braxton really already hired this guy?"

Jennifer raised her hands. "Your guess is as good as mine, but it wouldn't surprise me."

Wynne nodded. Braxton was the kind of client who did what he wanted and asked forgiveness instead of permission. Hiring a PI on his own was probably one of the more harmless things he could do when it came to his case, but still she would've appreciated having some input into the selection of the person they'd be working with.

A few minutes later, Jennifer buzzed her phone. "Your father is on line one."

Jennifer's words were simple and straightforward, but Wynne heard the lilting question in her tone. "Put him through," she said, willing her voice not to tremble. " While she waited for the call to connect, she stared at the phone like it was a snake poised to bite her. It had been several months since she'd spoken with either of her parents, and the last conversation had ended like so many others before, but the one thing she'd been able to count on was that they never called her at the office. Until now anyway.

"Hey, sweetie," the deep voice oozed through the line. "How are things?"

"Hi, Dad. I'm really busy right now."

"Of course you are," he replied, his voice starting to take on a slightly indignant edge. "I won't keep you."

"Okay." She waited, letting the beats of silence tick by until the inevitable happened.

"Your mother and I are a little short this month. It's nothing we can't make up in a few weeks, but the rent is due and there are a couple of repairs around the house that I can't handle myself. I was hoping you might be able to float us a loan. Not a lot, just a bit to bridge the gap, so to speak…"

His voice trailed off, and Wynne felt a familiar twinge of guilt for letting him ramble on since they both knew how this conversation would end. He called to ask for money, professing it would be a loan, and she would give him the money, knowing she would never see it again. Neither of them would ever reference repayment, and the next time he called, it would be a new day with new reasons why they were behind on rent, or the electric bill, or the car payment, or whatever. She would never ask for specifics about the cause of the gap, and he would never offer more detail.

"I'll transfer some money this afternoon. Anything else?"

"You mother would love to see you. Lunch on Sunday? It would mean a lot to her."

This part of the conversation, the part where the guilt was thrust back in her direction, was familiar as well, but after years of experience she was prepared with a response. "I have to work this weekend, but tell her thanks. I'll come by sometime next week." It was a vague promise, and one she wasn't likely to keep. They both knew it.

After she hung up, she went back to staring at the files on her desk, but she couldn't concentrate. Her mind kept wandering back to Campbell Clark, and she wondered if she too had a family she tried to avoid. If the rest of her family were as nice as Campbell's brother, Justin, then it wasn't likely. No, people like Campbell Clark had everything going for them from good looks to good family. Those kind of people had no idea what it was like to have to struggle for your dreams and fight to keep other people from stealing the spoils of your hard work.

Wynne pushed the file in front of her to the side, and a business card fell to the floor. She picked it up and stared at Lane's name and her cell phone number written in a flowing script. The loops and curls were downright flirty. Maybe she should give fun and flirty a try. Something to take the edge off. She reached for the phone and dialed Lane's number, ignoring the alarm bells clanging in her head. She waited impatiently through the rings, and when Lane answered, her voice was as silky smooth as Wynne remembered.

"I was hoping you'd call."

"Are you free tonight?" Wynne asked, surprised at her bold move.

"For you? Yes."

Wynne paused, knowing this was the moment when she should tell Lane what she had in mind, but this was as far as she'd planned, and on some level, she'd been prepared for Lane not to take her up on the last-minute invite. Her brain froze while she scrambled to come up with an idea, but Lane swooped in to save her.

"There's this wine bar I've been wanting to check out. You game?"

What Wynne knew about wine would fit on the head of a cork, but she'd committed to this lack of a plan plan, and she wasn't about to back down now. "Absolutely."

CHAPTER ELEVEN

Winebelly had an ultra cozy feel that wrapped Wynne in its warmth the moment she walked in, and she took the atmosphere as a good sign for the evening ahead. She smiled at the man behind the host stand.

"Good evening," he said. "Welcome to Winebelly. Are you on your own this evening or will someone be joining you?"

"I'm meeting someone." Wynne glanced around. "But it doesn't look like she's here yet."

"No worries. I can go ahead and get you a table, and I'll make sure she finds you when she arrives."

Wynne followed him back to a corner table after looking one more time over her shoulder when she heard the gentle bell of the opening door. She had to admit it was much nicer to say she wasn't here alone than her usual "Table for one, please," if only to avoid the sympathetic reaction of the waitstaff when they learned she was all on her own. Those typical reactions were the primary reason she didn't go out much. Of course, if Lane didn't show up, then things would be even worse than if she'd been planning to be here by herself. Anxiety buzzed through her and she began to form a contingency plan.

"Is this okay?" the man asked. "It's one of our more private tables."

"It's lovely." Wynne glanced back at the front door. No Lane. "I have to warn you though that my da…" She struggled a second for the right word to refer to Lane before deciding to skip over the reference entirely. "She may have to work late, so I may be on my own."

He set the menu on the table. "If that happens, we'll take extra good care of you." He motioned for her to take a seat and she did. While he spent the next few minutes reciting the wine list and the specials, including a few delicious sounding Mediterranean tapas, she focused on breathing deep and relaxing, enjoying the welcoming vibe and low-key energy of this little hideaway. If Lane didn't show, she'd be fine. Maybe this place would become her regular hangout. She'd never had one of those, but she liked the idea. In time, she'd come to know the man at the front door's name, and he and the rest of the staff would know hers. They'd swap stories about their day while she sampled new wines. She'd never been a big wine drinker, but she would learn. This place would become her place.

"Wynne, are you starting without me?"

She looked up, startled at the sound of her name, and saw Lane standing behind the host. Lane was dashing and gorgeous, and her grin was infectious, but Wynne couldn't help but miss the cozy, peaceful moment she'd been indulging in, and she wished she could get it back. She tried for a flirtatious tone to cover her disappointment. "Not a chance." She pointed her menu at the man. "My new friend, what's your name?"

"Zeke," he said with a smile.

"Zeke was telling me everything I need to know to create the perfect evening." She hoped she could remember some of what he'd said if quizzed on the point.

"Excellent," Lane said, edging past Zeke to slide into the booth. She took the other menu from Zeke. "I think I can take it from here."

Wynne watched as Zeke's smile lost some of its brightness at the obvious dismissal. He backed away from the table. "Just wave when you're ready to order and we'll send someone over to take care of you," he said.

"Okay, thanks." Wynne looked over at Lane who was running a finger over the choices. "I guess you've been here before and already know what you like."

Lane cocked her head. "Oh, I definitely know what I like, but it's not necessarily on this menu." She pushed it away and focused on Wynne. "I'm so glad you suggested this."

Wynne struggled not to squirm under her intense gaze. "Well, you suggested it first. And you picked this place, which I'm kind of in love with, by the way."

"Really? It's a little simple for my tastes. I was hoping they'd have a bigger selection. And tapas are so last year."

"So you haven't been here before?"

"No, but a potential client I've been trying to land told me this is his regular place, so I thought I'd give it a try. It'll give us something to talk about next time I give him a call." She pointed at the menu. "I'm sure I can find something suitable if you'd like to stay."

Wynne held back a frown. Barely. She wanted to stay, but she wasn't certain she wanted Lane to stay with her. She took a deep breath, and she could almost hear Seth in her head urging her to give the date more than five minutes before bailing. He was right. This was her first date in God knows how long, and she owed it to her potentially spinster future self to try harder, no matter how much she'd rather be home in her pj's knocking out some of the work that was piling up on her desk. "Let's stay. You can scope out the place, and maybe it will be better than you think." She smiled at the irony of her decision but hid her expression behind the menu. "I think I'll try one of these flights of reds." She ran a finger down the selections and decided to take charge. "Are you game for a cheese board? The yogurt I ate seven hours ago is no longer doing its job."

For a split second it looked like Lane was wavering, but then she closed her menu and slid it across the table. "That sounds perfect. But no Manchego, please. I don't care for it."

Wynne feigned nonchalance that Lane had dissed her favorite cheese, but she quickly brushed it off. Not everyone had the same taste, and she could eat Manchego on her own anytime. A waiter appeared and she placed their order, slightly disappointed that Zeke hadn't reappeared to take care of them.

"Why haven't we met before last week?" Lane asked in between sips of the first wine on the flight, a tasty Malbec.

"Because we're both workaholics?"

"I suppose, but I always make time for fun with pretty girls, no matter how busy things get."

Wynne felt the heat blush across her face. She'd never get used to being called pretty, and she didn't think she'd ever figure out how to respond to compliments about her appearance without sounding like a dork. She opted to brush past the remark. "I'd love to know how you do that. I can't seem to carve out time for a personal life."

"Combine the two. Like tonight for instance. We're here together and it's all about us, but bonus—I'm also getting a chance to check out a venue that might help me land a new client. It's the height of efficiency."

And super unromantic. Wynne winced at the thought as it shot through her. Since when did she care about anything romantic? Could be she was feeling a bit like everyone was using time with her to do something else, kind of like her trip to ACL with Campbell last week. But that trip had never been billed as a date. Apparently, she had some lingering frustration about whatever it was or it wouldn't have sprung to mind now.

Focus on the one you're with. Wynne shoved all thoughts of Campbell to the back of her mind and willed them to remain there. So what if Lane was efficient? There was a time when she would have admired the trait in a date. Hell, she was efficient, and she wouldn't mind if someone admired that trait in her. Determined to embrace the good things about this evening, she raised the second glass in the flight and injected as much flirtation as she could muster into her voice. "This one's the Sangiovese. Cheers to trying new things."

Lane raised her glass and met her gaze, her eyes twinkling with desire. "I'll drink to that."

Wynne sipped the smooth red and took a moment to let the liquid swirl on her tongue. She could make this work. Dating someone who had as big a workload as she did was smart. They could cheer each other on, respect each other's schedules, find a way to carve out time from business together. That they both worked for the same firm was icing on the cake. She took another sip of the delicious red and nodded her approval. This was going to work out just fine.

Campbell pulled up in front of Justin's house and smiled when she saw him watering their mother's rose bushes. When their parents had died, Justin had put his life on hold to be more than a big brother to her and their little sister, Perry, until they both graduated from high school and went off to college. During that time, he'd done his best to keep their home life steady, assuming all the around the house caretaking that her parents had done their entire lives, and he'd elected to stay in the big house even after she and Perry had moved away. She suspected part of the reason he stayed was for sentimentality, not just for what they'd lost, but a desire to re-create the close-knit home life they'd had with a family of his own in the future. In the meantime, they gathered here for special occasions and tonight was one of those.

"The roses are beautiful," she said, watching while he put away the hose.

"They are, aren't they?" He reached down and smelled one. "Last year the spring hail beat them down. Barely got to enjoy the blooms."

She slipped a hand in his. "You do good work, bro."

"Me and the sun." He pointed at the box. "What kind did you get?"

He reached toward her and she twisted to get away from his grasp. "You know the rule. Birthday girl is the first one to see the cake. Tradition."

"You sound like Dad."

"I confess, it's true."

"That's a good thing." She took his hand and led the way to the door. "Whatever you're cooking, I can smell it from here and it smells delicious." Birthdays at the Campbell house had always been a special occasion, and their mom had always insisted that no matter what plans they might make with friends, they had dinner with the family on the actual day, and the honoree got to pick the meal. She sniffed the air. "Is that mom's famous sauce? Are we having spaghetti?"

"Bingo. Now get inside because you're on pasta boiling duty. The birthday girl should be here in a half hour."

Despite his urging, Campbell took a few minutes to linger on her way to the kitchen. She stopped in the hallway and traced a finger along the frame of the last family photo they'd had made before their parents died. Her mother, Macy, had insisted they have a full family portrait made once a year, and she had the prior year's version at her house. They'd all groaned at the idea of dressing up for the photo shoot, and it had taken all of her mother's patience to corral them into the studio. Campbell shook her head. If she could get her parents back, she'd happily show up for the annual photo shoot. Every single time.

Justin was in the kitchen, stirring red sauce in a giant pot on the stove.

"The sauce smells amazing."

He dipped a spoon in and handed it her way. "I think I've finally got it down. What do you think?"

She moaned her response. It was delicious, and the tangy rich sauce brought a cascade of memories. Perry always asked for the same birthday meal—spaghetti. When Perry had been younger, there'd been meat balls, but now that she was vegan, they all deferred to a meatless meal on her special day.

Campbell reached into the cabinet for another big pot and set the water on to boil. When she announced it was al dente, Justin handed her a strainer, and she transferred the noodles to a bowl.

"We're all set," he said. "Let's get the birthday girl in here." He reached for a remote and powered up the TV mounted on the kitchen wall, and Campbell joined him in front of the television. A few minutes later, Perry appeared on the screen dressed in a wrinkled T-shirt and cargo shorts, and barely suppressing a yawn.

"What's the matter, kiddo?" Campbell asked. "Did we wake you up?"

"It's super early here. Can't a girl sleep in on her birthday?"

"And miss her favorite birthday dinner? Not a chance."

"It's tradition," Justin said. "Besides, I don't think Campbell is going to let me eat any of your birthday cake until you see it."

"Please say it's red velvet." Perry held both hands over her heart. "Even if I can't have any, at least I'll pine away knowing my siblings enjoyed my traditional birthday dinner."

Campbell opened the cake box and angled it toward the screen. "What are big sisters for if not the cake of your dreams?"

"I miss you guys."

The admission was huge. When Perry decided to spend her summer between law school semesters with a legal aid NGO in Afghanistan, both Justin and Campbell had tried to discourage her from traveling to the unstable country, but Perry would not be dissuaded. They'd finally settled on regular Skype sessions as a way to keep in touch and keep their worry at bay.

"We miss you too," Campbell said, coughing to cover up the fact she was choked up that Perry was halfway round the world instead of home on family birthday night. "We made spaghetti."

"Ha! You mean Justin made sauce and you boiled noodles."

"Sure, okay. But what about that cake?"

Perry held up a piece of flat bread. "You guys start eating, and I'm going to pretend this roht is a red velvet cake. Distract me from the illusion by catching me up."

Justin motioned for them to talk while he dished up the pasta. "Things are good," Campbell said. "It's been a little crazy trying to get things set up and get new business."

"Tell me everything," Perry said. "How are Abby and Grace? How's the new firm? Did you buy that table you wanted?"

"Abby and Grace are great. And yes, I got the conference table. It's gorgeous. Our biggest problem right now is finding a secretary who can take a message, and you know, spell, but we're working on it. I do miss not having to make personnel decisions and remembering to order things like copy paper, but eventually we'll get someone on board who can handle all those details for us." She started to tell Perry about the Leaderboard case but didn't want to have to explain how she kind of had their business, but not really. It was an in person, not Skype, kind of conversation.

"Glad you're making it work, but don't forget to get a life. If you're just going to work all the time, you may as well have stayed at Heartless and Done."

"Oh, she's making time for a personal life."

Campbell turned at Justin's announcement and punched him in the shoulder. "Am not."

"Are too," he said. "Perry, you should've seen this chick she brought to ACL." He fanned himself. "She was smokin'."

"You're the one who's smokin'," Campbell said, miming a joint pressed to her lips. "Don't listen to him, Perry. He's been spending too much time pretending to be a roadie, and he's lost touch with reality. Tell us what you're working on."

Perry woke up more as she talked, clearly excited about her current adventure, and Campbell was relieved to shift the conversation away from her. As she watched Perry and Justin talk about the rudimentary technology she was having to deal with in the remote village where she was staying, Campbell was struck by how lucky they were to still be so close even after such a devastating loss. She missed her parents with her whole heart, but Justin and Perry loved her and she loved them, and together they could handle anything life threw their way. Did Wynne have a family she could count on?

The question popped into Campbell's head without warning, like all her other not-very-professional thoughts about Wynne had lately, and she blamed it on Justin bringing up how she'd brought Wynne to ACL. Campbell watched Justin teasing Perry while Perry acted all cool, but Campbell knew she was a softie inside, happy to have a birthday dinner in her honor even if she couldn't be there to actually eat the food. If Wynne didn't have this, then she was missing out big time. But the real question was why did she care so much what Wynne did or didn't have in her personal life? Because if you knew your opponent's weakness, you could chart a path to their destruction. Sure, that's it. She knew it wasn't true the second she formed the thought, but the alternative was going to get her into trouble for sure, so she didn't even go there.

CHAPTER TWELVE

Wynne walked into the Leaderboard building and looked around the lobby, pleased to see she'd beaten Campbell to the meeting. She gave her name to Prairie and took a seat to wait. She would've preferred to conduct this meeting at her office, but everything about this case was determined to test the bounds of propriety, so why should this be any different? Under normal circumstances, the lawyers would have hired the private investigator directly to protect the attorney-client privilege, but she supposed they could work that out with the paperwork she'd packed for the meeting.

A few minutes later, Campbell burst through the door with a bright pink box in her hands, conjuring up memories of her presentation to the board. Was Campbell going to bring donuts to every meeting they had? Did she think sugar was the gateway to all things?

Prairie led them back to a smaller conference room than the one where they'd made their pitches before the board, and invited them to have a seat. "Brax will be with you in a few minutes."

Wynne sat down, pulled out a legal pad, and started jotting notes for the meeting while studiously ignoring Campbell.

"I don't think I'll ever get used to hearing everyone here call him Brax," Campbell said.

"Uh-huh," Wynne said, keeping her eyes on the paper in front of her. She totally agreed, but she wasn't going to get sucked into idle banter with Campbell. Their interactions from here on out would be completely professional and all about the case. But apparently, Campbell had other plans.

"These are the best apple fritters on the planet. The whole. Entire. Planet." Campbell shoved the box her way. "Trust me."

Wynne kept her hands folded on the table and barely glanced at the box. "I'm good."

"I'm sure you think so, but you will be so much better if you have one of these. Trust me."

"What if I were diabetic? Would you be pushing your big box of sugar on me then?"

Campbell looked stricken. "Are you? I'm sorry." She pulled the box back toward her. "I won't push sweets on you again, I swear."

Wynne nodded and looked back at her notes, which were really just scribbles because she was too distracted to write anything that actually made sense. After a few moments of silence, she started to feel bad for snapping at Campbell whose only crime was offering her a donut. "I'm not really diabetic."

"You're not? Well, that's good."

Campbell looked at her expectantly, and Wynne considered making up some other excuse for why she didn't take Campbell up on her offer. She sighed. "Carbs make me fat. And I know how this goes. If I reach in there and grab a donut, Braxton will walk through the door while it's hanging out of my mouth. I'll have sugar all over my face and on my fingers, and I'll look stupid and he'll fire my firm and I'll lose my job, and it doesn't really matter how fantastically magical those fritters are, they won't support me when I'm living on the streets."

She skidded to a stop and took a breath while she wondered where that rambling speech had come from. Now Campbell was going to think she was crazy. She wasn't sure why she cared, but she did. A beat of silence was followed by Campbell bursting into laughter. Figured. "It's not funny."

"Oh, it kind of is. The diabolical fritter plot. If only I'd known how easy it was going to be to steal this account right out from under you, I would have had a dozen jelly-filled wonders sent to your office weeks ago."

"Oh, no, not a fan of the jelly. Now, if you'd said Bavarian cream, then it would be war."

"Duly noted." Campbell made a show of making a note in her phone, and they both erupted into laughter. Wynne couldn't remember the last time she'd laughed so hard, but now she wondered why she didn't do it more often since it felt so good.

"What did I miss?"

They both looked up to see Braxton standing in the doorway of the conference room wearing a curious expression. Wynne immediately went into serious lawyer mode, but Campbell was still grinning. Wynne stood. "Hi, Brax. I hear you have a PI you'd like us to meet."

He looked confused. "I do, but I think at least one of you has already met her."

Now it was Wynne's turn to be confused, but before she could respond, Campbell jumped in.

"You hired Meg's firm?"

"I did," Braxton said. "Very impressive." He addressed Wynne. "Not that the names Stoltz sent over weren't impressive as well, but Meg Dunst has done a lot of work on cases in the music industry, and that gave her an added boost."

Wynne fixed a smile on her face, but her mind was racing. She had no idea who Meg Dunst was, but obviously Campbell did. And apparently, Stoltz had sent over his usual list of old white guys retired from government service whose ideas about investigative work didn't involve anything related to the digital age. Damn. She would have to get Jennifer to keep her posted on all communications between Stoltz and Braxton and do damage control where she could or this case was going to slip through her fingers. "I've heard great things about her," Wynne lied. "I can't wait to meet her."

"Great. She'll be right in. I'll say hello and then leave you all to get started. Just let me know if you need me. Are those Kate's donuts?"

Wynne followed his gaze and caught Campbell wearing a grin again as she pushed the pink box toward him. "They're the best donuts in Austin," Campbell said. "But you must know that since you have her captive here."

Braxton plucked one of the jelly filled gems from the box and sighed with pleasure as he took a bite. "She's not a captive, but we are. We have to walk by her every day, and the temptation is crazy."

"Has she always had mad baking skills?"

"Since we were kids. Used to drive our mother crazy because she could never keep the kitchen clean from Kate's experiments."

Wynne watched the exchange and realization dawned. "Wait, Kate the donut wonder is your sister?" She looked over at Campbell and was glad to see she looked equally surprised.

"That's where I recognized her from," Campbell said. "I read a post about her in *The Austinot* last year. They said her truck was a must-visit, but I've never seen her around town." She turned to Wynne. "Have you?"

"I'm afraid I'm not the person to ask when it comes to where to find the best donuts." Wynne saw Braxton raise his eyebrows, and she replayed the words in her head. "I mean, I'm sure they're fantastic. It's just that I don't eat a lot of donuts."

Campbell's laugh broke the tension. "I think Wynne eats more broccoli than donuts. I should probably be more like her."

"Shouldn't we all?" Braxton said.

The door to the conference room opened and a tall blonde strode in. "All I heard was broccoli and donuts," the woman said. "That's not a choice at all."

"Meg," Braxton said. "Thanks for coming. This is Wynne Garrity and I think you already know Campbell Clark."

Wynne extended a hand, pleased at the strong, firm grasp, but before she could say anything, Meg released her grasp and turned to Campbell.

"Campbell Clark, it's been a while, but you look as good as ever. Thanks for recommending me for this gig."

"Only the best for our best client."

Wynne wanted to roll her eyes, but Braxton smiled at the sentiment, so she smiled too to cover her irritation. Round one to Campbell. Whoever controlled the investigation would have a leg up on the case since the investigator would likely feel compelled to report to Campbell first. She made a mental note to figure out a way around that.

Braxton backed toward the door. "I'm going to leave you to it. I brought Meg up to speed on things from my end on the phone. If you need me, set something up with Prairie."

He was gone within seconds, and Meg slid into the seat beside Campbell. "Shall we get started?" she asked. "First item on the agenda is a question. Does anyone have dibs on that apple fritter?" Before anyone could answer, Meg reached across Campbell and plucked the fritter from the box while Campbell playfully beat her arm.

Wynne stared at the two of them, certain she was witnessing a layer of intimacy that went well beyond any kind of working arrangement. Had Campbell suggested Meg for the job because she was in a relationship with her? Did Braxton know? Her earlier irritation soared to new heights, and it took all her self-restraint not to pick up her things and go.

"What about you, Wynne? Not a fan of the donut?"

"Oh, she's a fan," Campbell said, "but I neglected to pick up the right kind. Won't happen again."

Wynne heard the trace of flirtation in Campbell's tone, but it only confused her again. Did she flirt with everyone? Why did that disappoint her? She shrugged it off. She wasn't here for donuts or flirting or anything else that wasn't related to defending Braxton's company from a lawsuit. Her firm had been here first, and they would still be handling Braxton's business long after Campbell, her pink box of goodies, and this tall, beautiful private investigator were long gone. Time to focus on business. "Glad to hear it. I actually have to be at another appointment later this morning. How about we get started?"

Campbell watched Wynne carefully. She was confused by her sudden change of mood when Meg came in, but she cared more about having the advantage in this case than she did about Wynne's discomfort. Or did she? The whole donut conversation had been strange. Who didn't like donuts? But when they'd finally relaxed into it, it was actually the first time she thought she and Wynne might get along. Until Braxton came in the room. Was Wynne really so concerned that any display of humanity would jeopardize her ability to keep Braxton's business? If that was the case, then perhaps the real question was whether she should take advantage of Wynne's vulnerability.

She didn't want to. She wanted to get along and win the case on her own merits, not by tearing someone else down. And the more time she spent with Wynne, the harder it was to deny their attraction, which made it even more difficult to treat her like any other competitor. But only one firm was going to come out on the winning side after this case. If she had to, could she make the difficult choice?

Too many questions. She needed to work all this out, but now was not the time. She squared her shoulders and assumed what she hoped was a serious, ready to get to work expression. "Meg, I'm not sure what Brax told you about the case so far, but basically Rhea Hendricks is suing Leaderboard, claiming a bunch of bogus causes of action boiled down to a claim that the site damaged her popularity and her chance at work in Hollywood. Our goal is to show that any damage to her popularity was her own doing. The site uses an algorithm to determine who makes the board, and Hendricks wasn't fulfilling the criteria." She turned to Wynne. "Does that about sum it up?"

Wynne looked surprised to be asked, but she recovered quickly. "Mostly. The drawback is that we don't want to get in a position where the only defense we have is to reveal the algorithm, because it's proprietary. If that's our only choice, then Leaderboard may as well file bankruptcy because there will be a dozen copycat sites out within days, not to mention it will tank the pending stock offering."

"So basically, we need to assassinate Rhea Hendricks's character," Meg said.

"Well, assassinate is a strong word," Campbell said. "More like articulate other legitimate reasons why she fell in the standings."

"Assassinate is okay with me," Wynne said. "Braxton is counting on a win. Whatever it takes."

Campbell stared at Wynne. She'd expect a hyper aggressive approach from Stoltz, but coming from Wynne, the forceful push surprised her. "How about this? You gather whatever information you can, and then we'll decide on the best approach?" She started to ask Wynne if that was okay by her, but she didn't want to hash out their different approaches in front of Meg.

They spent the next hour going over the list of potential witnesses she and Wynne had made of people they wanted Meg to interview. Meg made copious notes, and thank God, spent minimal time flirting. Meg's persistent and widespread charm was the primary reason she and Campbell had never developed a relationship past a couple of dates and a few shared sleepovers. It wasn't that Campbell was jealous, but she liked her dates to be focused on her instead of scanning the room like she had a serious case of fear of missing out. Despite the fact they no longer spent any intimate time together, Meg was the first name that came to mind when Braxton had asked her who she wanted to hire as an investigator. The same skills she used to seek out the next best thing in her personal life served Meg well when she was hunting down witnesses and schmoozing to get them to open up to her.

When they wrapped up their session, Campbell and Wynne packed up their files. Campbell was reaching into her bag, when

Meg touched her arm. "Are you busy tonight? I'd love to catch up and I owe you a nice tequila."

"Someone has a good memory," Campbell said.

"I make it a point to remember important things."

Campbell heard the sound of a throat clearing and turned in time to see a frown on Wynne's face before she looked back down at the file in front of her. "Actually, I need to work tonight. I'll catch you later." She watched while Meg walked out of the room and waited until the door shut behind her before addressing Wynne. "Sorry about that. Meg's a great investigator, but an outrageous flirt."

"Clearly."

"Does that bother you?"

"Does it bother you?"

Campbell rankled at the edge in Wynne's voice. "Answering a question with a question. Nice."

"My question is valid. If your...friend's flirtation is going to be a distraction, perhaps that's something you should've considered before you hired her to work on this case. Or maybe you owed her a favor?"

Campbell bit back a sharp retort. She knew when she was being baited, and she wasn't going to fall for it. Was it possible that Wynne was jealous of the attention Meg had laid on thick? "I didn't hire her. Braxton did. And as for distractions, nothing gets me off task when I have a goal in sight."

Wynne looked up, finally, and her gaze was penetrating. "I'll make a note of that."

"Good." Campbell said, unsure how to read Wynne's response. "I do plan to work on my half of the discovery responses tonight. Would you care to join me so we can knock them out together?"

Wynne pulled in her lower lip like she was thinking about it, but she shook her head. "I have other plans tonight."

"Hot date?" The words tumbled out before Campbell could stop them, but once they were out she held her breath for the response.

Wynne stood and shoved her papers into her bag. "Don't worry. I'll get my part of the work done. I'll email you my draft tomorrow."

Before Campbell could reply, Wynne was out the door. Campbell looked down at her notes. She had a ton of work to do and she needed to focus, so it was just as well that Wynne hadn't taken her up on her offer. She packed her briefcase and then stared at the last, lonely donut in the bright pink box. Telling herself it wouldn't do to let Brax see that any of his sister's donuts had been left behind, she wrapped it in a napkin for a midafternoon snack. Oh, who was she kidding. It would be gone before she reached her car.

Wynne dialed Seth's number, put her phone in the cup holder, and pulled out of the parking lot while it was dialing.

"Hey, girl, how're you doin'?"

She smiled at the sound of his happy voice. Exactly what she needed. "Better now."

"You sound like you're in a tunnel. Do you have me on your phone speaker?"

"Yes, I do."

"When are you going to get a car with a Bluetooth? The nineties called, and they want their flip phone back."

Normally, his teasing didn't bother her, but today it was like nails on a chalkboard. "I called you for advice, but I'm hanging up now."

"No, don't hang up. Is it about Lane? Because she mentioned that you had a date and all systems were go."

"I'm not even sure what that means," she said, surprised at his announcement since she would've ruled the first date no more than a four on a ten-point scale, and she certainly hadn't gotten any different vibe from Lane.

"I'm pretty sure it means she liked you. Did you like her back?"

"Next you're going to pass me a note and have me check off boxes."

"Or you could just tell me."

She wasn't quite sure how to approach this topic with him, having never called him with girl trouble before, and now that he'd brought up Lane, she didn't think she wanted to get into her whole day, including how agitated she'd gotten while watching Meg flirting with Campbell. "It was fine. She's nice."

"'Fine'? Ouch. She said she asked you out again, but you turned her down."

"I told her I had to work."

"You have a right to have a life, you know."

"I know."

"Then have one. Seriously, Wynne, billable hours aren't the only thing the partners consider when it comes time for promotion. Lane is on her way up and she's really well-connected at the firm."

"Are you telling me I should date her as a way to make partner?"

"Of course not, but I am suggesting that if you won't go outside the firm to have a personal life, then you could find one within that might make your professional life a whole lot easier to handle too."

His point echoed the exact same thought she'd had during her mediocre first date with Lane, but what he wasn't considering was what would happen to that professional life if she and Lane didn't work out. Things could get messy. Of course, she was borrowing trouble she didn't have. It was a big firm, and this was just a date. All she had to do was keep it casual. And it would be a way to keep her mind off of Campbell.

After she hung up with Seth, she contemplated her options. She could work alone. She could call Campbell and tell her she'd changed her mind. Or she could go out with Lane. If she tried to work tonight, alone or with Campbell, she'd only be distracted. Before she could change her mind, she pulled over and sent a text to Lane.

Is it too late to take you up on the offer for tonight?

She waited a few minutes for the buzz of an incoming text, but nothing happened. She started to pull back into traffic, but just then her screen lit up.

Eddie V's. Eight o'clock.

Wynne stared at the screen, trying to decide if she was attracted to the commanding nature of the text or put off by it. Before she could think it to death, she thumbed out a quick response. *See you there.*

She hoped she wasn't making a big mistake.

Chapter Thirteen

Wynne walked up to the hostess stand, but she spotted Lane already seated in a booth and told the hostess she'd find her own way. She took a deep breath and walked across the room, past tables of people engaged in lively conversation over decadent food. She'd been to Eddie V's for client lunches, but never at night, and the atmosphere was decidedly more romantic than businesslike. Definitely a date spot.

Lane's head was bent over her phone, and she was typing furiously with her thumbs. Work, probably, which was exactly what she should be doing. Seth's voice echoed in her head. *A girl's got to eat.* Lane didn't look up as she approached, and for a brief second Wynne wondered if she turned around and left would Lane even notice? She swallowed the thought and strode to the table. "Either you're writing the great American novel or there's a crisis at work."

Lane kept typing while she looked up and flashed a dazzling smile. "It could be both."

"True. Now that would make a good story."

"Are you going to sit down?" Lane's thumbs were still moving. "I swear I'll be finished in just a second."

"If you need to bag on me, I totally get it," Wynne said. "Believe me, I understand."

"I have no doubt you do, but I have no intention of bagging." Lane typed a few more strokes, and then set her phone on the table face down. "All done. Now join me or I'll start to get a complex."

Wynne slid into the booth, taking in the fact Lane already had a glass of wine. She tried for a teasing tone. "I see you've started without me."

"Just warming up."

Lane waved to the waiter and signaled for him to bring two more of what she was drinking. The presumptive act annoyed Wynne, but she chalked it up to Lane's strong personality. "Have you been here long?"

"About ten minutes. I figured I'd use the time to check in with my mother. She had surgery yesterday, and I knew it was only a matter of time before one of my siblings pointed out that I hadn't been in touch."

"Surgery? Is she okay? Does she live here in town? Do you need to go see her?"

Lane leaned forward and whispered. "Face lift and a tummy tuck."

Wynne stared, hoping her face was frozen in a mask of the concern she'd felt a moment ago. She felt stupid for all her questions now and wished she could reel them back in. Not that a woman didn't have a right to have plastic surgery, but having a mother who had that kind of discretionary income was so far out of her sphere of understanding that she couldn't comprehend. Wynne considered all the things she might do for someone who had just had surgery—make a casserole, bake some cookies. Not exactly appropriate for someone who'd just tried to eliminate the effects food had on their body. She settled on a simple, "I hope she heals quickly."

"Oh, she'll be up and around in no time. It's not her first time under the knife."

Lane waved her hand in the air as she talked as if mothers having plastic surgery was no big deal, and her nonchalance caused Wynne to think about her conversation with her father. She'd transferred the money as she'd promised, tempted to include more than usual in hopes it would be enough to tide them over for longer, but she knew better. Extra money would only open up new ways to part with it. A surefire home-based business, a penny stock on the verge of splitting, or something else that was guaranteed to be the "next big thing." Whatever it was, they would promise that their financial moves were calculated to build a nest egg and pay her back, with interest. She almost wished they would blow their money on something like plastic surgery because at least then they'd have something to show for it.

The waiter appeared with their wine, and Wynne took a deep drink to wash away the funk that always came from any interaction with her parents, so she could focus on her date. The wine was good, and she felt bad for her earlier irritation that Lane had taken control. "This is nice."

"It is, isn't it? I bought a case of this when I was in Napa last year, as well as a few bottles of the extra reserve. I should've bought more. Last time I checked Winebid, it was selling for four times what I paid, and I didn't exactly get it at a bargain. Have you been to Napa?"

Wynne had never heard of Winebid, and she was still processing Lane's wine math, but she struggled to catch up. "No. I can't remember the last time I went on a vacation."

"Oh, you really should. Napa's great, but I like Santa Barbara much better. There's this sweet little Danish town, Solvang, which is a perfect home base. You definitely want to hire a driver for the wineries—it's the best way to really enjoy your time there. I was thinking it might be a fun getaway for the weekend. I can't do it this weekend, but maybe next?" She pointed at her menu. "The portions are huge here. How about we start with the ahi tuna appetizer, and then are you okay sharing the misoyaki? I already had them put a bottle of Veuve on ice."

Wynne's head started spinning. Had Lane just asked her to go away for the weekend? She replayed Lane's words several times and decided that she had indeed asked her to go to Santa Barbara, although ask probably wasn't the right word considering she hadn't waited for an answer before plunging into an elaborate micromanagement of their meal. She thought back to the text Lane had sent her, not asking, but telling her where they would have dinner without bothering to find out if Wynne even liked seafood which is what Eddie V's was known for.

But it wasn't just their meal Lane was managing. Wynne had a strong sense Lane was used to handling all the women she dated. Not cool. Not cool at all. Her irritation grew as she imagined a weekend away, captive in wine country, with Lane telling her what wine she should drink, where they would stay, which wineries to visit, and God knows what else while she droned on about her mother's plastic surgery or some other nonsense. Wynne shifted in her seat, agitated at the prospect of spending another minute in Lane's company. Desperate to escape, she pushed her wine glass a few inches away and made a show of touching her forehead. "I hate to say this," she lied, "but I have a colossal headache. Guess I shouldn't have skipped lunch," she said, ending on an honest note.

"Oh no," Lane said, her voice laced with concern. "We should get you something to eat."

She held her hand in the air to signal the waiter, but Wynne tugged on her arm. "I think I might have passed that point. I think I just need to lie down."

"Of course. I'll drive you home."

Wynne's gut twisted. She hadn't planned this escape very well. "No, please stay. I can make it home. I think I just need a good night's sleep." She stood. "Please, I insist."

Lane didn't offer again, and although Wynne was glad, she filed away the fact under reasons why Lane was the center of her own universe. Wynne offered to pay for her wine, but Lane declined and Wynne didn't push the point.

When she left the restaurant, there was a nice breeze—unusual for a summer night—and she was grateful she wouldn't spend the next couple of hours hearing all the extravagant details of Lane's super cool life. She slipped behind the wheel of her ten-year-old Honda Accord and contemplated her options. Work was definitely on the table, but the office was out of the question on the off chance Lane decided to stop back by. Work at home it was. She started the engine and glanced at the dashboard clock, surprised to see it was still early. Before she could contemplate the complexities of what she was about to do, she turned in the direction of Campbell's office and dialed her cell.

"I didn't expect to hear from you tonight," Campbell said without preamble.

"Are you still working?"

"I am."

"Great. I have some ideas. I'm headed your way. We can talk when I get there. See you in a minute."

Wynne started to click off the line, but Campbell yelled, "Wait."

"What?"

"Where exactly are you headed?"

"Your office. Why?"

"Because I'm at my house."

"Oh, well, never mind. We can talk tomorrow." Wynne wished she'd ignored her earlier impulse and just gone to her own house in the first place.

"Nonsense. My place isn't far from the office. I'll text you the address."

Campbell hung up before Wynne could respond, and once again she was left contemplating her options. She could go home and work or go to Campbell's and work. She didn't spend long deciding. Work was work, and if she saw where the enemy lived, she might get some intel on how to take her down. Wynne heard her phone buzz with an incoming text and made her decision on the spot.

Campbell's house was a cute Craftsman, not much bigger than her own bungalow and not far from hers either. It was cornflower blue with yellow shutters and a wraparound porch lush with a variety of plants. She wondered if like her house, Campbell's had been in the family or if Campbell had paid the exorbitant prices that Austin transplants nonchalantly shelled out for housing. Wynne parked in the driveway and walked to the front door. She knocked and was surprised when the door immediately flew open, and she stood face-to-face with Campbell who was wearing a UT law school T-shirt and Nike shorts, keyword short.

"Hello," Campbell said, sweeping her arm in welcome. "Come in and get comfortable. Rule number one of being self-employed. You can work at home in your pajamas or your sweats whenever you want. Or at least whenever you don't have client meetings." She turned and starting walking back into the house. Wynne paused for a moment in the doorway, her gaze trained on Campbell's toned, bare legs, wondering whether she'd made a mistake coming here. If the amount of time she was spending staring at Campbell's legs was any indication, she should run in the opposite direction.

Campbell popped her head around the corner, and Wynne jerked her head up to meet Campbell's curious eyes.

"Are you coming?" Campbell asked. "I made snacks. Tasty ones."

Wynne nodded. There was really no way to bow out gracefully now. Besides, she'd already ditched one woman tonight, and as a consequence, she was starving. "Lead the way."

Campbell's kitchen was small but well equipped. A six-burner gas stove, a KitchenAid mixer, and various other expensive appliances gave the impression she was a consummate chef. Not what Wynne would have expected. She ran a finger along the edge of the candy apple red mixer.

"Don't you just love that magical machine? Justin gave it to me for my birthday two years ago when I told him I was going to start baking to relieve stress. Of course, I don't know if it's a good stress reliever because I've been too busy to use it. I found this recipe for profiteroles I want to try though. I'm committed to making that happen."

"You like to cook?"

"You sound surprised."

"I am. A little. I mean…" Wynne didn't want to finish the sentence now that she'd started. "I know you're a donut eater in public, but in my experience, skinny people have refrigerators full of nonfat yogurt and lemon water. And kale. There's always kale." Campbell wrinkled her face. "Not a fan. Of kale, that is. I love yogurt, but the kind that comes in those cute little glass jars that I'm fairly certain contains all the fat that was removed from the creepy nonfat kind. What's your secret?"

"What?" The question threw Wynne who was busy being embarrassed at the fact she'd mentioned Campbell's appearance again.

"You have a killer body. Do you run or spin or what?"

Wynne felt her ears warm and prayed the blush hadn't spread to her face. "Coffee. I live on coffee. Black. It's my superpower."

"Well, it does a good job." Campbell's gaze slowly scanned her from head to toe, and Wynne tried not to squirm under the inspection. "But tonight there will be kale-free snacks. I'm having wine to go with. Does that work for you?"

Wynne's mind traveled back to the restaurant where she'd left Lane sitting with two almost full glasses of wine on the table. Probably very expensive wine if Lane's preferences were any indication. The idea of sharing wine with Campbell was so much more inviting. "That sounds perfect."

Campbell reached behind her and grabbed an open bottle of red. "I tried this at a local wine bar, Winebelly. It's one of my favorite places, and the sommelier recommended this blend on my last visit. I loved it so much I bought a case."

"I love that place," Wynne said. "It's so cozy and inviting."

"I know, right? I spend way too much time there. I'm kind of surprised I've never seen you there."

"I've only been once, but it made a really good impression." Wynne made a vow to go back to Winebelly sometime in the near future, and not with Lane.

"So, how was your date?"

"What?" Wynne wondered if Campbell had read her mind.

"You said you were too busy to work tonight, remember? But you're here kind of early, so I'm thinking that your hot date was a bust."

"There wasn't a date." Wynne figured there was truth enough in that statement since showing up at a restaurant and listening to Lane talk about her wonderful life until it gave her a headache shouldn't count in the date column. But it wasn't the whole truth, and she felt bad about fibbing, although she had no idea why she thought she had any duty to share the details of her evening with Campbell. Before she could think it through further, she blurted out, "That's not true. I was on a date. Or it was supposed to be a date, but it wound up being a bust."

❖

Campbell had been half kidding when she mentioned Wynne's plans for a hot date, but she couldn't deny the sense of relief when Wynne said her date had been a bust. *Play it cool.* She reached for the tray of snacks and motioned for Wynne to join her in the living room. "Did you at least get to eat dinner?"

"Not even. I feigned a headache before I was halfway through a glass of wine."

"Ouch. Well, I can fix the hunger part. Try this cheddar with this fig and olive cracker. It's a flavor combo that will not only stave off hunger, but will make your heart sing." Campbell watched while Wynne arranged the cheese on her cracker just so, and then crunched down on the creation, followed by a gentle moan. "See?"

Wynne pointed at the rest of the cracker. "Perfection. I'm officially addicted after just one bite."

"Join the club." Campbell took a sip of wine to gather courage before she plunged back into the subject of Wynne's evening. "Was this a blind date?"

If Wynne was surprised at the personal question, she didn't show it. "Actually no. It wasn't even a first date. We met for drinks once for a casual let's meet and talk. Tonight was supposed to be the real date with dinner and stuff. All I got was a few sips of wine. Truly excellent wine that she insisted on ordering for me. I probably should've asked for a to-go cup."

Campbell wanted to ask about the "and stuff," but she resisted the temptation. "Okay, so you'd already had some experience with her?"

"Yes, but you know how sometimes you write off first impressions by telling yourself first times are usually awkward and that you should give things a bit more time before you give up on them?" She waited for Campbell to nod. "Not the case here."

"It was worse?" Campbell hoped she didn't sound as pleased as she felt.

"Uh, yes. Don't get me wrong. This woman is beautiful, and on paper she's the perfect catch, but she is well aware of all her attributes and she likes to talk about her wonderful life. A lot. It was a bit much."

Campbell tried not to focus on the "woman was beautiful comment," and instead raised her glass. "But she has good taste in wine."

Wynne touched her glass to Campbell's. "Yes, but so do you."

The comment hung in the air for a moment like it was buoyed by the weight of its implication, and they locked eyes for several long moments. Finally, Campbell cleared her throat and stood. "Speaking of wine, I could use a refill. Are you good?"

Wynne held her gaze for another second. "I am surprisingly good, but I'd love another glass."

Campbell walked into the kitchen and opened the door to the fridge and stuck her head in to cool off. She didn't need another glass of wine. What she needed was a distraction from the way her body reacted whenever Wynne was around. Before it had been easier because Wynne's caustic personality was at odds with her wildly attractive vibe, but tonight she was drinking wine and eating cheese and crackers like a person who actually enjoyed life and might be fun to hang out with. Campbell knew she had to be careful not to fall into thinking they were anything other than rivals. She couldn't afford to forget the future of her firm depended on winning Leaderboard's business, and she owed it to Abby and Grace to remember where her loyalty belonged. Determined to stay on track, she poured a glass of ice water for herself and brought it along with Wynne's refill to the living room. "Ready to get to work?" she called out as she walked into the room.

Wynne was standing in front of the fireplace, looking at the pictures on the mantel. "Are these your parents?"

"Yes," Campbell said, avoiding eye contact. Fresh off Perry's birthday dinner, her emotions were raw when it came to thinking about her folks. She pointed to the coffee table strewn with papers. "I made some notes about a motion for summary judgment. I think if we have a good plan of attack ready, we'll know what questions we should ask at the depositions to support the motion, and then it'll only be a matter of inserting the supporting facts to fit the legal arguments."

"Uh-huh. Sounds good." Wynne set the frame back on the mantel. "Are you close?"

"What?" Campbell struggled to follow. She saw Wynne glance back at the photo. It was one of her favorites, from when she was ten years old. Her parents had been dressed up for a Valentine's Day date night, leaving her and Perry in Justin's care for the evening, despite their protests. She remembered her dad telling her it was tradition to take the love of your life out on Valentine's Day, and that one day she'd be dressing up for the same tradition. She sighed when she remembered that this past Valentine's Day, she'd spent the evening eating takeout Chinese at the office, preparing for a deposition the next day. Thank God her dad couldn't see how pathetic her love life had wound up becoming. "Yeah, we were a pretty close-knit family, but my parents died when I was in high school, so now it's just me, Justin and our little sister, Perry. Still close, but I miss those two something fierce."

Wynne placed a hand on her arm. "I'm so sorry."

Campbell brushed away a tear. "You don't have to be. They were great, and I'm lucky to have had parents who loved me no matter what and believed I could be anything I wanted to be or do anything I wanted to do, even if I didn't have them for very long."

Some people have parents who live forever but never love them the way my parents loved the three of us."

Wynne nodded like she was listening, but her eyes were hooded and she seemed distant. Fresh off baring her own soul, she risked a personal question of her own. "Are you close to your family?"

Wynne turned sharply and her eyes narrowed for a second before a neutral mask fell into place. "We get along okay." She walked back to the couch. "Care to share your notes?"

Okay, so apparently there wasn't going to be any reciprocity where personal issues were concerned. Campbell filed that nugget away and took a moment to arrange her papers into something resembling organization. "I've made a list of all the factors that go into the Leaderboard algorithm." She pointed at the handwritten chart she'd composed. "The columns to the right represent the witnesses who should have testimony to offer to either support or disprove that particular factor." She ran her finger down the page. "Check this out. This guy is Rhea Hendricks's wedding planner."

"I knew she was engaged to Dash Wilder, but I didn't realize they'd gotten to the wedding planning stage before they broke things off."

"Yep. She was all in on that relationship. And here's the thing—Dash is still wildly popular. I'm thinking that when they broke up, her score on Leaderboard tanked because most of her connections were Team Dash. In fact, I think that once we get all the discovery responses, we'll see that she took a hit across the board once news of their breakup went public."

"And the wedding planner is going to say what exactly?"

"A wedding planner is a lot like a priest. They're present during all the big decisions. What kind of ceremony to have, who to invite, how much money to spend—you get the point. He's going to have some insight into whether or not Rhea was a bridezilla. If she was, you can bet there are other people she pissed off who in turn stopped connecting to her on Leaderboard. The more support we can show for why her Leaderboard connections were abandoning her, the easier it will be to assert that no matter what the algorithm was, she was losing popularity on the app simply as a reflection of her real life."

"How do you know so much about weddings?"

"*Say Yes to the Dress? Bridezillas? Whose Wedding Is It Anyway?*" Campbell paused, waiting for some signal Wynne was following.

"I feel like I'm supposed to know what you're talking about, but I don't have a clue."

"I'm guessing you don't watch much reality television."

"Make that TV period. Who has time?"

Campbell heard the undercurrent of judgment and took a breath before responding. "I think it's important to be in touch with modern culture. Take this case for example. Are you on Leaderboard?" she asked, already knowing the answer.

"Uh, no. Seriously, it's just a big popularity contest."

"Judgmental much? Yes, it's a popularity contest, but popularity wins you influence, and clients, and success. I bet your firm makes you go to bar networking functions where you all stand around with watered down drinks and not great snacks, awkwardly jockeying for business referrals. Remove the bad drinks and snacks and you have Leaderboard. And bonus, you can make connections while in your pajamas if you want."

"You're really into this whole pajama thing."

"You're making fun of me."

Wynne smiled. "I'm not really. And you're right about Leaderboard. I guess I just thought it was a place for all the popular people to fawn over each other."

"Have you even checked it out?"

"Enough to learn the basics."

"Well, that's not going to work. Someone needs a deep dive tutorial." Campbell opened her laptop and set it between them. "Do you want to set up your own profile or do you want me to do it for you?"

Wynne pushed the machine back toward Campbell. "I'm good."

"Ah, someone likes to shy away from the limelight." Campbell nodded. "I get it. You like to be stealthy. That's one approach and I respect it." She watched relief flood Wynne's eyes and decided she was on the right track. "How about I take you through my profile to give you a sample of what's in store, and then you can decide if you want to jump into the Leaderboard pool on your own later?"

At Wynne's nod, she set the laptop back between them and entered the URL for the Leaderboard site into her browser. She looked at Wynne to see if she was following along, but Wynne's eyes were fixed on her, not the computer, and they were smoldering. Campbell stared back, barely breaking their locked gaze to take in Wynne's parted lips. They were red and full and lush, and Campbell suddenly had a strong desire to trace her tongue around Wynne's tantalizing lips, and she started to lean in, but just as she did, Wynne jerked her head away and pointed at the screen.

"You're connected to Kevin Bacon? The actor?"

"What?" Campbell said, scrambling to get her mind back in the game, but her heart was racing. Speaking of connections, had she just imagined that on the edge of a kiss moment? Had she imagined that Wynne felt it too? "Wynne, I—"

"Are you dodging the question, counselor?"

Campbell studied Wynne's face, searching for any sign she hadn't imagined the current that had passed between them, but Wynne wouldn't meet her eyes. She wanted to ask Wynne if she was the one dodging things, but what if she was wrong and speaking up only made things between them weirder than they were already? Talk about awkward. She plastered on a smile. "I must confess that I do have a connection to Kevin Bacon. Justin made me go with him to a Bacon Brothers concert in Houston last summer. He had backstage passes, courtesy of his pals at ACL, and," she raised her hand, "this hand got to shake Kevin's. The rest is history."

"Seriously?"

"Cross my heart. I doubt he remembers me. He probably only accepted my request to connect because of Justin."

"That's a great story." Wynne shook her head. "You're not what I expected."

"What did you expect?"

Wynne shook her head, her cheeks showing a faint blush. "Never mind."

"Nope. There will be no dropping of comments like that without follow-up. Talk to me."

Wynne twisted her hands in her lap. "You were so popular in school, and you had such a tight group of friends. I guess there was a part of me that figured you had it easier than the rest of us, but it's pretty clear you're smarter than I ever gave you credit for, and now that I said that out loud, it sounded much more rational in my head. Can we just forget I said anything?"

"In a minute." Campbell replayed Wynne's words, and she stuck on the way Wynne had said "popular" like it was a bad word. "You thought I was stuck-up, didn't you?"

"Maybe a little. You guys were definitely the in-crowd. I don't think you even knew the rest of us existed."

Campbell looked down at her hands and thought back. Almost every memory she had of school was of her and Abby and Grace and their group of friends. They'd studied together and partied together, cried on each other's shoulders, and planned their futures together. She knew plenty of other people in her class, but she hadn't formed close relationships outside of her group. But hadn't everyone else been that way too? "You didn't have a group of people you hung out with?"

"Sure, but much smaller, and we were never part of the in-crowd. You and Grace and Abby were at the center of everything. Everyone wanted to be part of your study group, or just hang out with you. You were like law school rock stars."

"Talk about an oxymoron." Campbell laughed, but she had questions. Lots of them. Topping the list was whether Wynne had wanted to hang out with her back then. But the bigger question was whether she would've wanted to hang out with Wynne. Back then, probably not. She remembered Wynne, always serious, always studying. She never joined them at happy hours, never showed up for parties. In her mind, Wynne had always been too studious, maybe even judging them for having fun. "I remember you always hanging out with Seth Greer. You and he were always studying together in the library."

"Yep, me and Seth, the center of our own little universe."

Campbell heard the sadness in Wynne's voice. She wasn't sure of the source, but felt partly responsible. She reached over and grasped Wynne's hand. "I'm sorry we weren't friends back then."

"I'm sorry I said anything. It's silly really," Wynne said. "That was a long time ago."

"Five years isn't that long."

"I guess not."

"We can be friends now," Campbell said hopefully.

"Friends who are trying to kick each other's asses in a battle to the death for the client of the year?"

"Yes, that kind."

"Yeah, okay, that works for me."

Campbell smiled, but she was the tiniest bit conflicted between being happy they'd reached a truce of sorts and the settling for just friends status, but she knew this was for the best. Now that the angst was out of the way, hopefully, the strange attraction she had to Wynne would go with it. They would be friends, working hard on a case together. If only they weren't working against each other too.

CHAPTER FOURTEEN

"Y ou were at her house? Where does she live? Is it beautiful? It is, isn't it? Tell me everything."

Wynne swatted Seth with a copy of the state bar magazine and put a finger over her lips. "Stoltz is lurking. Shut the door."

Seth complied and settled into a chair, leaning forward expectantly. Wynne took her time arranging things on her desk, stalling for something to say and wondering why it seemed so hard to slip into their usual gossip mode. Before he'd walked in, she'd been staring off into space thinking about Campbell. Which was a big problem since she should be thinking about the case. But every time she opened a file and tried to focus, the images of Campbell, comfortable and casual in her element, popped into her head, and she replayed every moment of last evening, including Campbell's very kissable lips and how close they'd come to crossing a very uncrossable line.

Seth tapped his fingers on the desk, breaking her out of her dreamy state, and she scrambled for words. "Not much to tell. She lives near South Congress, and her house is about the same as mine."

"Oh, I guess I expected she would have someplace palatial. Word on the street is that she's bankrolling her firm, and they don't even need the Leaderboard business. They want it mostly for PR."

"Don't believe everything you hear. That doesn't even make sense. Why would they need PR if they didn't want new business?"

Seth shrugged. "Just telling you what I heard. If the rumors are true, you should be on the lookout for her to break out something really flashy to impress Brax."

The idea of friendly, kissable Campbell from last night surprising Braxton with a litigation version of a flash mob left Wynne feeling agitated, and she cast about for a new subject that didn't have anything to do with Campbell Clark. "How have you been? Working on any big cases?"

"Matter of fact, we just signed a new digital services client. They've got a bunch of new patents, and Lane's going to be working with me on getting them licensed." He leaned back in his chair. "Speaking of Lane, want to fill me in on your big date before I see her and get her side of your budding romance?"

Wynne resisted protesting the term "budding romance," because she didn't want to get Seth started on a litany of all the reasons why Lane was perfect for her. She decided to keep her response simple and partly true. "Uh, it was nice."

"Didn't you go to Eddie V's? I love that place. Their ahi tuna appetizer is my kryptonite."

Wynne fiddled with some papers on her desk, avoiding eye contact. She remembered how Lane had gushed over the tuna appetizer, and she felt a slight twinge of guilt that she'd fled the restaurant before they'd even ordered. Lane probably thought she was a total flake. She'd texted her the next day to apologize and Lane had replied asking her if she was feeling better, but neither contact was prolonged, and Wynne figured Lane was as done with her as she was with Lane. She toyed with making something up to tell Seth, but they'd always been honest with each other no matter the consequences.

"I didn't stay for dinner."

"Was it just drinks then? Sort of a reconnaissance mission?"

"I didn't exactly stay for drinks either. I left early. I said I had a bad headache."

"But you didn't?"

"Nope. Well, kind of. I mean sometimes listening to someone drone on about themselves gives me a headache." She sighed. "And in the interest of full disclosure, I left and that's when I met Campbell to work on the Leaderboard case."

"At Campbell's *house*. At night. With wine and snacks."

Wynne raised her hands. "All true. I confess there were snacks. And wine. Probably not as good of snacks as there were at the restaurant, but snacks they were."

Seth crossed his arms. "Hmm."

"You obviously have something to say. Out with it."

"You realize she's off limits, right?"

"Who?" Wynne tried not to wince at her own insincerity.

"You know who. Campbell Clark is not our kind of people."

Wynne wanted to protest and tell him he didn't really know Campbell, that the Campbell Clark they thought they knew in law school wasn't that person at all, but she didn't want to risk raising his suspicions by protesting too much. "You're imagining things. There's nothing going on between us."

"You keep telling yourself that. In the meantime, you should remember that you never liked her and you're competing for the same client. Only one of you can win, and trampling your enemy doesn't make for a very good start to a relationship."

Wynne turned Seth's words over slowly in her mind. Trampling. Enemy. Relationship. She wasn't trampling anything. More like she'd been won over to Campbell's easygoing style. And enemy was a strong word for what should be a professional competition. But it was the last term—relationship—that had her hung up the most. As long as she and Campbell were working together on this case, they'd have a working relationship, but she was certain that wasn't what Seth meant. She started to set him straight, but something kept her from it. She had a feeling that something was Campbell's smile or the way her legs looked in her short shorts. Either way, she was in trouble for sure.

❖

Campbell balanced the cake box on her hip and shoved her way through the door of their law offices.

"Hey."

She looked up to see a handsome, dark-haired stranger sitting behind the reception desk. "Who are you?"

"Excuse me?"

"Who are you?" she repeated, her irritation growing as the box started to slip from her grasp. She dropped her briefcase to the floor and managed to catch the box with both hands, while handsome guy stared at her like her little show was solely for him entertainment.

"I'm Graham Bunn, with two n's, the new head of client management for Clark, Keane, and Maldonado."

Campbell shook her head, wondering which of her pals had hired this one. "Well, Graham, I'm Campbell Clark, yes, that Clark, and I don't need to be managed, but I do need you to get out of that chair and help me carry this stuff into my office."

He hesitated, casting a glance back toward the interior of the office as if he thought he should check with someone to make sure she was really who she said she was, until Campbell stamped her foot in frustration. "Right, then," he said, "Let's get you all tucked away." He strode over and easily handled the cake box and her briefcase. Campbell led the way to her office, scowling at Abby whose open door she passed on the way. She pointed at her desk, and Graham obediently set her stuff down. He'd barely left when Abby appeared at her door.

"So you met Graham?"

"You mean the new head of client management? I wasn't aware we had enough clients to manage."

"I told him to stop saying that. I'll talk to him again. You'll be happy to know he can spell and appears to be able to speak in complete sentences."

Campbell sank into her chair. "That's an improvement from the last one. Please tell me you'll talk to him about the title? And maybe he doesn't have to tell everyone his name is Bunn, no matter how many n's it has."

Abby laughed. "I'll talk to him, but please let's give it until the end of the week before you decide you can't stand him. If I have to interview one more wacko, I'm going to go back to my old firm where at least I didn't have to deal with a parade of crazies."

"I thought Grace was in charge of this little project," Campbell said.

"I think we broke her. She's meeting with the landlord to go over the list of things that still need to be fixed around the office. How goes all things Leaderboard?"

"Okay, I guess."

"That doesn't sound great. What's up? Any way I can help?"

Campbell glanced back toward the door to make sure Grace hadn't suddenly appeared and that Mr. Client Management wasn't lurking. "It's a lot harder than I thought it would be to work with Wynne."

"Really? I mean I know she's super focused, but she seems friendly enough." Abby ducked her head and narrowed her eyes. "Do you feel like she's out to get us?"

Abby's remark was loaded with layers of meaning. Campbell figured it was unintentional, but she needed to share what had happened between her and Wynne, even if it was just to get the crazy feelings out of her system. "We almost kissed."

"What? Who almost kissed?"

Cursing her for being momentarily dense, Campbell said, "Focus. Me and Wynne."

"You and Wynne? There was kissing?"

"Almost kissing. Completely different than actual kissing."

"Right. I'm going to need more details." Abby made a show of looking at her watch. "And a drink. Stat."

"It's barely lunchtime." Campbell pointed at the box on her desk. "Will profiteroles do?"

"You brought cream puffs?"

"Correction, I made cream puffs. I used that mixer that Justin gave me. It's kind of amazing."

"You must really like this girl."

"What did you say that for? I didn't make her baked goods."

Abby reached into the box and pulled out a perfect profiterole. She gazed at it lovingly for a moment, and then sank her teeth into its crusty layers, emitting a soft moan. "This is perfection. You can pine away after all the girls you want if it means you'll keep bringing stuff like this to the office."

"There's no pining."

"Right. I forgot. There was actually kissing."

"There wasn't any of that either. But it was close."

"How close?"

Campbell closed her eyes and relived the moment. "Lips parted, breath bated, dreamy eyes close."

"But no actual flesh on flesh?"

Abby's question inspired a rather graphic image of Campbell's lips pressed against Wynne's, and her mind roved to other places. Where were their hands? Were their bodies pressed together? Eyes open or shut? The room suddenly seemed really small and super warm. Shit, she needed to get her mind off Wynne, and fast. "No. No actual touching occurred." She paused while her mind cycled back through the evening. "I may have touched her hand once."

"Casually or all hey, baby, let's take this a little further?"

"Eww, I'm not a cast member of *Baywatch*. I'm sure it was casual. But it was nice."

Abby wagged a finger. "I've seen that look. You're in trouble."

"Am not."

"Exhibit A: Nina Hawkins."

Campbell sighed. Nina Hawkins had been in her third year when they entered law school, and she'd been assigned to Campbell, Abby, and Grace as their mentor, which was how she and Grace had met Abby. Nina had captured her attention from the moment they met, and Campbell had an unrelenting crush on her for the rest of the school year. She wanted to protest, tell Abby that this wasn't the same thing at all. Wynne wasn't a mentor, and she wasn't a starry-eyed first year law student, but she couldn't deny the hazy, dreamy feeling whenever she thought about Wynne was pretty much the same as the one she'd felt about Nina. Damn. "Well, you'll be pleased to know that just like with Nina, this isn't going anywhere."

Abby reached out and clasped her hand. "Probably for the best. Wynne seems nice, but it would complicate things. I promise there's someone out there for you, and when things settle down, I'll do whatever I can to help you find Ms. Right."

"Promise me you won't use the same set of skills you used to hire the new head of client management."

"Deal." Abby rose and grabbed another cream puff before she left. Campbell watched her go, torn between being grateful she had such good friends and feeling regret that she hadn't told Abby everything, because although there'd been no touching, she'd wanted there to be, and she was still disappointed she hadn't taken advantage of the moment when she'd had the chance.

Chapter Fifteen

Wynne paced the conference room at her firm for the tenth time, making sure every chair at the table had a water glass, a pad of paper, and a pen. Today's deposition, the first in the case, was a show of power, not just to the wedding planner who they were about to depose, but to Braxton who'd decided to attend. Campbell's small firm might have a stylish table, but stylish wasn't formidable. Stylish didn't convey the weight of dozens of years of experience being brought to bear to crush the claims of the unrighteous.

Okay, maybe that was a bit much, but Wynne was determined to show everyone involved in this case that her law firm was the one best equipped to take down the opposition. She'd spent hours preparing meticulous lists of questions, and she was ready to show Braxton that his business belonged with Worth Ingram.

But this fierce determination, which usually filled her with excitement, was bittersweet because the opposition was Campbell, and she knew she'd made a mistake by mixing personal and professional time with her. *You shouldn't have cozied up to her. Big mistake.*

The voice in her head was right, but she wasn't sure what to do about it now except maintain her distance. Hard to do when they were about to be sitting next to each other for the entire day.

"They're here."

Wynne turned around at the sound of Jennifer's voice. "Did Rhea come with them?" The parties to the suit didn't have to be present, but she wanted to be prepared just in case.

"No, just her fleet of attorneys. Mr. Keith, the court reporter, and Campbell are here too. Do you want me to show them back?" Wynne nodded, but as Jennifer turned to walk away, she changed her mind. "Actually, send Rhea's lawyers to the library, and ask Campbell to wait in my office while the court reporter gets set up in here."

A minute later, Brian, the court reporter, entered the conference room, and she walked him through her seating arrangement so he could set up accordingly. When she was done, she smoothed her skirt, straightened her jacket, and marched to her office, prepared to put all of her pesky, unprofessional feelings about Campbell Clark behind her.

It wasn't easy. Campbell was standing in her office looking like she'd walked off the pages of a fashion magazine called *Glamorous Lawyers* or *Legal Legs for Days* in a mid-thigh black skirt and white suit jacket with black trim around the lapel and pockets. In contrast, Wynne felt like an undertaker in her plain, no frills, black suit. Campbell looked up as Wynne entered the room, and Campbell's face broke out into a wide smile, but Wynne resisted the urge to fall into the warmth of it. She took a deep breath and shut the door behind her. "We need to talk."

Campbell grinned like she thought Wynne was teasing. "Sounds ominous."

"I know I was the one who showed up at your house, and ate your snacks, and asked about your parents, and…" She looked at the wall past Campbell's shoulder, then the floor, anywhere to avoid direct eye contact for fear she would lose her nerve. "But we need to keep our relationship strictly professional."

"Okaay." Campbell drew the word out. "Have I done something to offend you?"

If only. Wynne could handle contentious battle. It was the friendly foe that scared her most. She'd started to let her guard down, and after that night at Campbell's, more walls had fallen in the face of friendly Campbell. She could live with that, but the almost kissing? No way she could let that possibility continue to hang in the air between them without losing complete and total focus on her ultimate objective: keeping Leaderboard's business and trouncing the competition.

But she couldn't tell Campbell any of this without admitting exactly how undone their causal closeness left her. "No, you haven't, but I think it's important for both of us to remember that although we're working on this case together, we're in competition." She managed a humorless smile. "It'll be less painful when I take back all of Leaderboard's business."

Campbell smiled too, but it was cautious, and the sparkle in her eyes had dimmed. "I see." She moved toward the door. "You'll be sorry when you're craving some of my special snacks." She opened the door. "Oh, and, Wynne?"

"Yes?"

"I've decided to take the lead on the deposition. See you in there."

Wynne watched the door swing shut behind Campbell, too dumbfounded to reply, not that it would matter if she had since Campbell was no longer in earshot. "The hell you are," she muttered under her breath. She grabbed her binder full of her detailed notes and rushed out of her office, but before she could make it to the conference room, Braxton appeared in her path, holding two bottles of what looked like mud.

He shoved one of the bottles toward her. "Beet juice? I hear it's going to be a long day."

She hid a grimace and reached for the foul looking liquid. "Thanks." How could the same guy who let his sister have a donut food truck on his work campus be so attached to vegetables with all the life sucked out of them? "I have a couple of last-minute things to take care of, but if you want to wait in my office, I'll come back and give you a rundown of how today's going to go."

"I'm good. Campbell just filled me in on the main points. So, you'll be taking notes while she asks the questions? For some reason I thought maybe you two would each get to question the witnesses?"

Wynne faked a smile and glanced around, looking for Campbell who she was about to strangle. Her only saving grace was that Stoltz was out of town today on a last-minute trip for a client that couldn't be rescheduled. If he returned to find out Campbell had stolen this opportunity, there would be hell to pay. "Actually, only one attorney for each party is allowed to question each witness. Campbell and I are still working out all the details. In fact, I should speak with her again before we get started." She edged toward Jennifer's desk. "Excuse me."

She found Campbell in the conference room, chatting up Brian, the court reporter, like they were long lost friends. Figured. They both looked up as she entered the room, and she pointed at Campbell. "A moment, please."

Brian looked between them and excused himself from the room, shutting the door behind him. Wynne barely waited for the door to close before she stalked toward Campbell. "I've spent the last week living and breathing every aspect of this case in preparation for this depo. We had an agreement."

"It was a coin toss. Hardly a well-reasoned debate," Campbell said, stepping forward into her space.

They were close now. So close, Wynne could feel the hum of electricity between them, and it was all she could do to keep her cool while Campbell's lips were inches away. "We agreed." The simple phrase was all she could manage. She should back away, gather her wits, and try again, but she was powerless to break free from the tractor beam of attraction.

"What will you give me if I let you do it?"

Wynne heard the words, but she lost the context in the haze of Campbell's spell. "What?"

"I'll make you a deal. I won't fight you for this depo, and I only have one request in exchange."

Still hazy, Wynne waited for the catch.

"Have dinner with me tonight. To discuss the deposition, to discuss the next one and the one after that—I don't care. You can pretend it's whatever you want, but I pick the place and you let me take you. Deal?"

Dinner with Campbell would be dangerous. No way could she stay focused on business, and not only that, but she was about to spend the entire day with Campbell. By the time dinner rolled around, she'd be completely distracted, unable to extract an ounce of let's get this done.

But she was powerless to resist. "Okay."

"Okay?" Campbell stared hard. "You're not just saying that to get your depo back, are you?"

"What difference does it make if it means you win?"

Campbell's eyes dimmed for a second, and for the second time since she'd arrived, Wynne knew she'd offended her in some way. Campbell shrugged. "It doesn't."

"I'll go." Wynne blurted out the words before she could change her mind and was oddly pleased at her choice. Campbell raised her eyebrows, and Wynne rushed to reassure her. "I want to go. But someplace casual, okay? It's going to be a long day."

"Sure," Campbell said, a hint of her enthusiasm showing through. "And don't act like you've been sent to a firing squad. I promise to pick something we'll both like."

Wynne nodded, forcing back a smile. The deposition was starting in five minutes, leaving no time to bask in the glow of Campbell's invitation, which was just as well. She'd already forgotten the name of the wedding planner, which meant even the idea of dinner with Campbell was a distraction she couldn't afford, but for the first time in her life she wasn't interested in shutting out her personal life for her professional one. *It's only dinner.* It wasn't and she knew that, but she was determined to get through this deposition, and then she'd figure out what came next.

❖

Things were going better than Campbell could've imagined. The wedding planner had all kinds of dish about Rhea's rocky relationship with Dash, and Wynne was skilled at getting him to make admissions before he figured out where her questions led. She passed a few notes to Wynne with suggested questions, but for the most part, she didn't think she could've done a better job, and a part of her was attracted to Wynne's skill.

She'd known Wynne was smart, but getting witnesses to open up like this was next level skill, and Wynne had it in spades. Brax had nodded his approval several times during the day, and Campbell knew that should put her on guard, but instead she just felt a sense of pride, like this woman she was drawn to was not only pretty, but smart too. Dangerous, but she vowed to not let her personal feelings affect her own performance at the next deposition. No matter what happened on their date tonight.

Date. This was really happening. She needed a plan. Place, time, date clothes. Campbell looked down at her suit. It was one of her favorites, one she'd picked up for a sweet deal at Neiman's, but nothing about it fit Wynne's request for causal. She glanced over at Wynne's carefully constructed deposition outline, and then at the clock on the wall. At the rate they were going, they'd wrap this up in time for her to run home and change. Her favorite jeans were clean, and she could pair them with that new top and sandals she'd ordered online last week. Although wearing brand new shoes for the first time probably wasn't a great idea. Her mind wandered to slipping out of her shoes, and then—

"Objection."

The loud exclamation was punctuated with slammed fist on the table, tearing Campbell from her first date fantasy. Rhea's attorney was standing now, towering over the court reporter. He pointed at the wedding planner. "Don't you dare answer that."

Campbell silently cursed her lack of attention, and she looked at Wynne to try to clue in to what question had set off this firestorm. True to form, Wynne had her forefinger on the current question in her notes, the apparent absence of any written contract between

Rhea and the wedding planner. Wynne shook her head. "Objection noted. Please answer the question," she told the wedding planner.

"Don't you do it." Rhea's attorney, Jeb Lawson, was leaning across the table now, his imposing bulk looming.

"Let the record reflect counsel for the plaintiff is standing and leaning over the witness," Wynne said to the court reporter. She turned to Jeb. "Do you have a specific objection you'd like to note for the record or are you just posturing?"

"I've let him answer your gossip questions, but he's not permitted to discuss the exact terms of the contract he had with my client. He needs to keep his mouth shut or he's in violation of his nondisclosure agreement."

Now completely out of fantasy mode, Campbell whipped out a copy of the requests for discovery they'd filed along with the deposition notice and tossed them on the table in front of Jeb. "It sounds like you just admitted that a written contract exists. Do you want to explain why you didn't produce it in response to our requests?" When both Wynne and Jeb stared at her, she said, "What?"

"Are the two of you planning on tag teaming all the witnesses?" Jeb asked with a sneer. "Because I can bring along an associate to bully your witnesses if you want."

Campbell raised her hands in surrender and shot an I'm sorry look at Wynne. "Sorry, just trying to help. Ms. Garrity has the floor."

Wynne didn't betray any hint of annoyance. She picked up the carefully tabbed document and handed it to the witness. "We're still on the record. Please show me in this contract where it says you agree not to disclose certain aspects of your arrangement with Ms. Hendricks."

He set the papers on the table. "It doesn't."

"All right then. Let's talk about—"

"I signed the nondisclosure for Mr. Wilder."

Campbell scribbled a note and handed it to Wynne who barely glanced at it before shoving it behind her notes. "I think this is a good spot for a quick break," Wynne said. "I'm requesting that the witness not speak to either side during the break, and we'll resume in fifteen minutes." She was out of her chair before she finished talking, and Campbell swept up their notes and rushed to follow her back to her office. She didn't wait for an invitation to enter and shut the door behind them. Wynne was already behind her desk, typing on her computer, and Campbell waved a hand in her face. "Hey, care to share what you're up to?"

Wynne looked surprised to see her standing there. "Just running a few quick searches in WestLaw about enforcement of nondisclosure agreements."

"Would probably help if we actually had the agreement. Lawson obviously withheld it."

"I'm not sure Rhea can enforce the provisions of a contract between two other parties." Wynne clicked a few keys, and a list of cases appeared on the screen in front of her.

"But this guy can refuse to answer based on that agreement," Campbell said. "If I were representing him, I'd tell him not to answer."

"Sure, but he didn't bring his own counsel, and Rhea's attorney has no business advising him what to do." Wynne pointed at the door. "I was kind of hoping you would stay out there and keep an eye on things. Make sure Lawson doesn't try to intimidate the witness."

"You know, you could have told me that's what you wanted."

"What?" Wynne's eyes were still glued to her computer screen.

"Look, I know we're in competition here, but neither one of us is going to get Leaderboard's business if we tank this case. You've got the lead on this depo, and I'm your assist. Let me help you."

Wynne tore her gaze away from her computer, her expression skeptical. "You mean it?"

"I do. Let's win this together."

"Okay." Wynne stood. "I'll take another stab at the questions, and if he won't answer, I'll certify them for the judge. Does that sound like a good plan?"

"Exactly what I'd do. We can draft a motion to compel his responses tomorrow."

"We should probably go ahead and draft it tonight."

"I'm going to veto you there. I think the attorneys in this case have plans tonight, and if said plans are cancelled, it would result in you being in violation of your own agreement." Campbell watched as Wynne looked wistfully at her computer. "I promise we'll work on it together in the morning and have it filed before noon. Deal?"

Wynne hesitated only a moment. "Deal."

Campbell followed Wynne back into the conference room where Wynne asked a series of questions which the wedding planner, following Lawson's advice, refused to answer. Wynne asked the court reporter to certify the questions, which simply meant that she marked them for transcription so that they could file a motion asking the judge to force the witness to answer. While Campbell watched the exchange, she was already writing the motion in her head and scribbling a few notes to get them started tomorrow because she was going to have her uninterrupted evening with Wynne, and nothing, not even this case, was going to get in the way.

Chapter Sixteen

Wynne stood in front of her bedroom closet mirror and frowned. She'd insisted on casual, but faced with limited choices, she was beginning to second-guess. She'd worn jeans the night Campbell had taken her to *Austin City Limits*, and her mind wandered back to Campbell checking out how they fit. She supposed she could wear them again, but she only had one pair she liked, and if Campbell had been paying as close attention as she seemed to be, then she'd probably notice.

She started sweeping every hanger in the closet aside, frustrated by the presence of over a dozen suits and tailored blouses and not much else. She could hear Seth's voice in the back of her head telling her it was because she never did anything for fun. He wasn't wrong. Counting her dates with Lane, she'd been out more times in the last few weeks than she had been for the last two years, but tonight was different. For the first time in a long time, she was truly excited about doing something that didn't have anything to do with work.

She finally settled on tan slacks and a cornflower blue sleeveless blouse. After a quick look in the mirror, she let her hair down and brushed it out so it hung in waves around her shoulders. There—she was now ten times more casual than an average day, and she'd be appropriately dressed if Campbell didn't show up in those short shorts she was wearing the other night.

A quick look at her phone told her she had less than ten minutes to finish up. Enough time to rummage through the kitchen to see if she had anything suitable to offer Campbell to drink when she arrived. It didn't take long for her to realize her hostess skills needed some serious help. One bottle of expensive Scotch she'd won in a raffle at the last firm holiday party and an ancient bottle of champagne a client had sent her years ago after a big win. Hopefully, Campbell would want to go straight to dinner.

Wynne's phone buzzed and she looked at the screen, hoping Campbell was here to put her out of her pre-date anticipation misery, but it wasn't Campbell, it was her dad. Wynne instinctively reached for it, but stopped short of answering. She'd transferred the money like she'd promised but broken her word about coming by to see her mother, which would make for a longer conversation than she had time for right now. She started to fire off a text promising to call back later, but experience told her if she opened the lines of communication, the back-and-forth could go on for a while. For all he knew, she was busy at work, so she let the call go to voice mail and vowed to call him back tomorrow.

As if to signal her decision was the right one, the doorbell rang. Wynne took one last look at herself in the reflection of the microwave and strode to the door. Ready or not, she was going on a date with Campbell Clark.

Campbell sped toward Wynne's house with the windows down. She'd considered leaving the top down, but she didn't peg Wynne for a top down kind of girl. In fact, she'd been surprised that Wynne had suggested casual for this evening since the only other time she'd seen Wynne in casual clothes had been their trip to ACL. Even the night she'd dropped by after her aborted date, Wynne had been dressed like a lawyer. Did Wynne dress like that for all her dates? Campbell let her mind wander, and from there it was an easy jump to wondering what the other woman had been like and what was Wynne's usual type.

She was still daydreaming when her phone rang and Grace's number appeared on the dash display. Considering where she was headed, she thought about not answering, but decided that was a jerk move. "Hey, Grace," she said. "What're you up to?"

"Nothing yet. I'm here with Abby and we've decided we all need a night of cocktails. We haven't seen you all week. You can tell us all about the case, and we can fill you in on some firm biz. Are you still at the deposition? Should we pick you up?"

Campbell ran through her options. She could lie and say the deposition was running late or she could beg off and tell them how it had gone and say that she had to work on the motion to compel which was sort of true. She settled on vague. "I'd love to, but can I beg off tonight? I have to do a thing. Next week when the depositions are over? First two rounds will be on me."

"Are you sure?" Abby this time. "The new bartender at Charlie's is super hot, and word on the street is she's single. I say we draw straws for who gets the first chance to ask her out."

Campbell's stomach sank with guilt, but it was too late now to confess she was already seeing a super hot woman tonight, so she stuck to her original plan. "Rain check? I promise I'll make it up to you both. I'll even pass the bartender your number like the awesome wing woman I am."

"Sure, no problem. Next week. It's a date."

Campbell disconnected the call and tried to ignore the pit in her stomach. She didn't remember ever lying to her friends and certainly not about a girl, but she couldn't possibly tell Grace after her reaction before, and whenever she did get around to telling her, she wanted to be able to gauge her reaction in person.

She didn't have time to ruminate about it much longer before she pulled up in front of Wynne's house. When she knocked on the door, Wynne called out, "Be right there." Campbell shifted from one foot to the other, wishing she'd driven around the block rather than showing up early. Poor form, Campbell, poor form.

A few moments later, the door swung open and Campbell sucked in a breath. Wynne was beautiful every day, but laid-back Wynne was next level.

"You're early."

"I am. I'm sorry."

"Don't be." Wynne pulled the door open wider. "I'm almost ready. Do you want something to drink while I finish up?"

Campbell followed Wynne into the house, noting that Wynne had invited her in, unlike the last time she'd been here. "A glass of water would be great, but I can get it if you just show me the kitchen."

Wynne hesitated for a second before answering. "Okay, if you don't mind."

"Of course not. Can I get you something while I'm in there?"

"I'm good." Wynne led her to the kitchen. "Help yourself to anything you see, although I'll warn you I don't have much on hand," she said before disappearing into the back of the house.

Campbell found a glass, filled it from the faucet, and walked back into the living room. Wynne's house was smaller than hers, but nicely furnished. The furniture was either new or hardly used, and unlike her own place, it was pretty much devoid of anything personal, like photos or knickknacks. It was also squeaky clean, and Campbell wondered if Wynne spent her free time cleaning or if she had a maid service. On her salary at Worth Ingram, she could certainly afford one, and it made sense not to waste what little free time she had cleaning house. Campbell grimaced. She'd had a maid service the entire time she'd worked at Hart and Dunn, but if their firm didn't start having a regular cash flow, she might have to take a break or risk blowing her inheritance living the life she'd grown accustomed to.

"Did you find what you needed?"

Campbell turned at the sound of Wynne's voice to see her standing close. "You should always wear blue. It's definitely your color. I meant to tell you that when I walked in, but…"

"But it seemed like a weird thing to say to someone you're working with."

"I guess. I mean, I wouldn't normally hesitate to tell another woman they looked great, but this seems different."

"Could be the way you look at me when you say it," Wynne said with a sly smile.

"I suppose. Does it bother you?"

"Not really, no."

"Then how about we go out and not let anything bother us tonight?" Campbell waited for Wynne's answer, hoping she hadn't blown their evening with her inability to keep her feelings under wraps.

"Sounds like a good plan."

They spent the drive talking about their respective neighborhoods and how they'd had to deal with changes with the influx of so many new businesses and their employees who'd relocated to the area.

"It's great for business," Wynne said. "But all my new neighbors want to tear down the houses that have been around for decades and build bigger places with no character whatsoever. It's a constant battle."

"I hear you," Campbell said. "I bought my house near South Congress for the neighborhood charm, but there's a big difference between a natural funky, laid-back vibe and trying too hard to be chill. Last weekend, I walked to Jo's to get a cup of coffee and nearly tripped over some bearded hipster dude parked on the sidewalk with a typewriter. He offered to write me a poem on the spot. Sometimes I think the transplants take the 'Keep Austin weird' slogan too literally." She slowed down as they approached their destination. "Oops, this place is a lot busier than I thought it would be tonight. Help me look for a place to park."

Wynne smiled. "You're taking me to Winebelly?"

"You said you'd only been once and you liked it." Campbell spotted an empty space and steered her car in. "I hope it's okay."

Wynne placed a hand on hers. "It's perfect."

Campbell squeezed her hand, happy she'd chosen well. "Shall we go drink all the wine and eat all the tapas?"

"I can't think of anything I'd rather do."

❖

Wynne followed Campbell into the wine bar and immediately spotted the host she'd seen on her previous trip, Zeke. He greeted them both and then focused on her. "It's good to see you again. Is your other friend joining you?"

Campbell looked at her with a confused expression, and Wynne shook her head, certain he was referring to Lane. "No, just a table for two."

Zeke led them to a cozy table in the corner and gave them the rundown on the specials, encouraging them to try a new blend that had just arrived. They each ordered a glass, and after he walked away, Campbell said, "I thought you'd only been here once. You must have made quite an impression."

"Actually, it wasn't that long ago, which is probably why he remembered me."

"Was it a date?"

Did she detect a trace of jealousy in Campbell's question? "Prelude to a date. It wasn't great. And then there was the actual date. You know, the one I ditched when I showed up at your house."

"I remember it well. Her loss is my gain."

"Here's to that," Wynne said, looking up as Zeke approached with their glasses of wine. "You have perfect timing."

"Would you like to order some food or shall I give you a minute?" he asked.

Wynne inclined her head toward Campbell to let her choose.

"Let's take our time," Campbell said. "We'll give you a shout when we're ready." When he walked away, Campbell reached a hand across the table and grasped Wynne's. "I hope that was okay. I know we both barely had any lunch, but I'd like to savor a few minutes alone with you without feeling like there's a thing we have to do or a place we need to be."

Wynne looked at their joined hands, and then back up into Campbell's dreamy eyes. She could get lost there—a fact she'd known for a while now, but was just now beginning to surrender to. The implications were enormous and complicated, but she didn't want to think about them right now. She didn't want to think at all. She raised her glass. "Now for a proper toast. Shall I do the honors?"

Campbell held up her glass. "Please do."

"To seeing past the obstacles and living in the moment," Wynne wasn't sure she believed the sentiment, but if Campbell was willing to try, she was too.

Campbell tilted her glass toward Wynne's, and their glasses clinked to signal their relationship had shifted. Wynne took a sip of her wine and enjoyed the warmth of the alcohol trailing down the back of her throat, but along with it came a sense of agitation. It wasn't the wine, which was delicious, but she shifted in her seat, unable to get comfortable while she tried to figure out what had her on edge.

"Are you okay?"

She looked up at Campbell who was staring intently at her with dark and smoldering eyes. "Yes. I mean no. I'm sorry. I don't know what's wrong with me."

"You look flushed." Campbell raised her hand to signal the waiter. "Let's get you some water."

Wynne closed her eyes and did a mental check-in. The heat she'd felt after drinking the wine was spreading, enveloping her entire body. It wasn't the wine; it was the woman sitting in front of her. This pretty, witty, smart woman who'd remembered that she'd mentioned this wine bar and who'd brought her here in the most thoughtful of gestures. The edge she felt was the slippery slope, the crest of the mountain, the what-am-I-getting-myself-into realization before jumping into thin air.

"Let's get out of here," Campbell said.

"Really?" Did Campbell mean what she thought she meant? Wynne searched her face for clues.

"Absolutely." Campbell leaned forward, her expression sexy and determined. "We can drink wine at your house and order a pizza."

"I don't have any wine."

"I don't care about the wine."

Wynne stared into Campbell's eyes. They were piercing with promise, and in that moment, Wynne's agitation was swept away. She didn't care about wine, or dinner, or the case, or anything else beyond the bubble that was her and Campbell and whatever magic was happening between them right now. "I don't either. Let's go."

CHAPTER SEVENTEEN

Campbell watched Wynne fumble to fit her key in the front door lock and wondered if it was nerves, and if it was, were they good nerves or bad ones? Twice, she started to reach out to help but kept pulling back, torn between wanting to rush and wanting to take things slow, even if taking it slow meant Wynne changed her mind. Whatever was about to happen, they both had to agree or it would never work.

She heard the lock click. Wynne opened the door and looked back at her, her eyes questioning. Campbell took her hand and followed her inside. They both stood in the small entry, about a foot apart, like they were each waiting for the other to make the first move.

"I know you said you don't care about wine," Wynne said, "but I do have a bottle of Scotch that I'm sure is very old and expensive and a bottle of Champagne that may or may not be devoid of bubbles. I can get you a glass and—"

Campbell stepped close. "I'm good." She slipped an arm around Wynne's waist and gently tugged her closer. "Unless you want something besides this." She leaned forward until her lips were almost grazing Wynne's and whispered, "Is this okay?"

Wynne answered by capturing her lips between hers and holding them for an infinite moment before dipping her tongue into Campbell's mouth. Campbell moaned with pleasure, not even trying to contain her emotions as the delicious pressure between them built. The kiss broke naturally, and they were each breathing heavily after.

"Do you want to sit down?" Wynne asked, her eyes dark with desire.

"I have a whole list of things I want to do right now, but sitting isn't one of them." Campbell braced for Wynne to pull back in response to her enthusiasm and was pleasantly surprised when she didn't. Instead Wynne reached out her hand.

"I think we should work our way through your list," Wynne said as she led them back to her bedroom. Campbell was surprised that the room looked more homey than the rest of the house, with several framed photos and other personal items scattered around the room. She wanted to ask about the photos. Were the people family or friends? Currently in her life or from another time? But she didn't want to break this high voltage current between them, so she focused on the bed, which was surprisingly fluffy and feminine with a pale yellow comforter and about a half dozen cozy pillows. She'd expected Wynne's style to lean more towards Spartan, considering the rest of the house. She glanced over at Wynne to catch her staring. "Nice bed."

"You look surprised."

"I might be. Just a little." Campbell pulled Wynne close so that they were standing in each other's arms. She leaned in and kissed a light trail up Wynne's neck, ending near her ear. "Here I find out you're all boss in the boardroom and princess in the sheets."

"How long have you been waiting to use that clichéd line?"

"A long time," Campbell said with a grin. "So is it true?"

Wynne stepped closer. "Kiss me."

Campbell didn't hesitate. She pressed her lips to Wynne's, lightly at first, but then she increased the pressure, teasing with her tongue until Wynne opened to her. The heat ramped up as their lips melded, and Campbell ached to be even closer as she trembled with arousal. When their kiss broke this time, Campbell felt like she might melt into the floor if Wynne weren't holding her.

"Let's get in bed."

Wynne murmured the words against her neck, her jagged breath an intoxicant, and Campbell followed her across the room, surrendering to her control. Wynne stopped at the edge of the bed and placed her hands on Campbell's chest before taking an excruciatingly long time to unbutton her shirt. Campbell pressed into her hands, willing Wynne to move faster even as she savored the buildup. By the time Wynne finally pushed the shirt back from her shoulders and unfastened her bra, Campbell was hyper aroused, and when Wynne dipped her head down and licked along the edge of her breast, she became a quivering mess.

She reached for Wynne's shirt, running her fingers along her waistline, desperate to feel skin on skin. "Off," was all she could manage, and Wynne's face slid into a slow smile as she paused to remove her own top and bra. "Is that what you wanted?"

Campbell traced Wynne's dusky rose nipples with her fingers, enjoying the way they grew hard against her touch. "Yes, but this is only the beginning."

"Is that so?"

"Most definitely." Campbell leaned back against the pillows. "Weren't you saying something about getting into bed?" She watched as Wynne tugged off the rest of her clothes, stepped out of her own, and climbed onto the bed.

"Better?" she asked.

"Much," Campbell said, barely able to breathe at the sight of Wynne's slender naked body hovering over hers. "You're beautiful." Wynne started to shake her head, and Campbell reached up to stop her. "I mean it. Absolutely gorgeous. Inside and out."

"Yeah? Well, so are you." Wynne leaned down and traced her tongue along the edge of her breast. "So pretty," she whispered before sucking Campbell's breast into her mouth. Wynne's tongue was both soft and firm against her taut nipples, and Campbell writhed on the bed, desperate to get even closer when she felt Wynne's fingers between her legs, tracing trails of ecstasy along her thighs stopping only to dip into the wetness between her legs.

Campbell could sense her control slipping away, and as much as she wanted this to last, she wanted to surrender more. "I want to feel you inside me," she gasped, surprised she could speak at all. Wynne gently slid her fingers in, easing them in and out. Campbell matched her breathing to the slow, steady strokes and relaxed into the sexy rhythm of Wynne's caress.

Wynne's voice floated through the air. "I want to taste you."

"Please." When Wynne's lips grazed across her clit, Campbell shook with desire and completely relinquished control, arching up off the bed, willing Wynne to take her. Stroke after stroke, Wynne granted her desire, taking her to the crest of arousal and easing her back down again, over and over. Campbell fisted the sheets and rode each wave, finally letting go when she felt her orgasm build to a perfect pitch, sending her soaring over the edge.

The first thing Wynne noticed the next morning when she rolled over in bed was that she was alone. The second was that sunlight was pouring into the room. She stretched into the warmth of the sun's rays, enjoying the feel of her tender muscles, muscles she'd spent most of the night using in a way she hadn't in a long, long time. But she couldn't truly relax because Campbell wasn't here and she should be, because if she wasn't then last night was nothing more than a one-night stand where one participant slinks away in the dead of night and they never speak of it again.

Panic set in. They would have to see each other plenty while working on this case. How were they supposed to work together when every time she looked at Campbell memories of the hours of steamy, passionate sex filled her brain like they were doing right now.

Work. Wynne opened her eyes wide, staring at the natural light flooding from her window, and reached for her phone. It was after nine. She hadn't slept this late since...well, never. They were supposed to be up early, working on the motion to compel. She'd wanted to write the motion last night, but Campbell had talked her out of it. We can work on it tomorrow, she'd said. We have plans, she'd said. But now it was tomorrow and the morning was half over.

At that moment, Campbell tiptoed into the room wearing a robe and carrying a tray. Wynne squinted. It was the robe she kept hanging in the bathroom, and Campbell looked incredibly hot in it, which was problematic considering she had to get up right this instant.

"You're up," Campbell said, sounding disappointed. "I was letting you sleep in, but now that you're awake, how about coffee and breakfast tacos? Cream, no sugar, right? And I got several kinds of tacos. You can have first pick."

Wynne watched while Campbell set the tray on the nightstand, unable to fully process what was happening. "You went out for breakfast? In my robe?"

"Just to Jo's. I'm sure you know this, but your refrigerator is kind of lonely. Oh, and I wore clothes, but I spilled coffee on my pants and I rinsed them out and put on your robe. I hope you don't mind. "

"Not at all. You should always wear a robe, and nothing else." Wynne eyed the tray. "I don't really eat breakfast, but I'm pretty excited about that coffee."

Campbell sank onto the bed beside her and handed her a foil wrapped taco. "Consider it dinner, which we never wound up eating, by the way."

"True. Remind me not to believe you next time you offer to buy me dinner in exchange for a favor."

"Regrets already?"

Visions of Campbell—naked, on her back, writhing and begging for more—flooded her brain, and Wynne shook her head. "None. Last night was incredible." She reached up and ran her hand along Campbell's face. "You were incredible. My only regret is that we have to rush out of here." Campbell's brow furrowed, and Wynne added, "The motion? The one we were supposed to work on early this morning and file by noon?"

"Oh, yeah. About that." Campbell grinned and handed Wynne her phone, pointing at the screen. "It just needs a once-over and it's ready to go."

Wynne scanned the paragraph she could see and kept scrolling through page after page of sound legal argument supported by on point case law. When she was done reading, she handed the phone back to Campbell. "Let me get this straight. After hours of insanely good sex resulting in two orgasms—"

Campbell raised her hand. "Three. I counted at least three. And those were just the rock the walls ones. There were also all those aftershocks, which I quite enjoyed, by the way."

"Duly noted." Wynne laughed and shook her head. "After all that and no dinner, you woke up before the crack of dawn, composed a legal brief, including citations, on your phone, and then brought me breakfast?"

Campbell shrugged. "It's no big deal. You just looked so peaceful sleeping that I hated to wake you up."

"I don't remember the last time I ever slept this late." She stretched her arms over her head, but the usual creaks were replaced by a relaxed, languid feeling. "And I gotta tell you, it feels pretty good."

"Then enjoy it. Drink your coffee, eat your breakfast." Campbell held up her phone and stood. "I'm going to get dressed and take this to the office. I'll have it formatted and ready to file before noon."

Wynne watched Campbell walk across the room to where her clothes were folded neatly in a chair—another task she must have accomplished in the predawn hour. Every step Campbell took in the opposite direction chipped away at her newfound sense of relaxation and happiness. "Don't go."

Campbell turned and waited, but Wynne hadn't thought past the elemental need for Campbell to stay. Her brain started spinning. "I can email the motion to Jennifer, and she can get it formatted and filed. And then…" Suddenly, it occurred to her that maybe Campbell wanted to leave. She had a life, things to do. Maybe this had been a one-night stand to her. Lord knows they hadn't discussed what any of this meant.

"And then?" Campbell asked.

Wynne paused. She'd been trained not to ask a question if she didn't know the answer, but that was for work and this wasn't. She had no idea how these feelings about Campbell fit in with her future, personal or professional, but she did know exactly what she wanted in this moment. She wanted Campbell Clark, all to herself.

"And then you can stay here. With me." She patted the bed beside her. "Right here."

Campbell's face burst into a big grin. "There's nothing I'd rather do."

Chapter Eighteen

Campbell walked into her firm lobby, surprised to see Graham Bunn had managed to survive his first day and was back behind the receptionist desk.

"Greetings, Ms. Clark," Graham said, his voice bright and cheery. "I placed some mail on your desk, and mere seconds ago you received a call from a Wynne Garrity with Worth, Ingram, Nash, and Reed. She asked that you contact her this afternoon, but she specified it was not an emergency. I have her number here. Shall I type this information up and email it to you?"

Any other day, Graham's over-the-top formalism would have gotten on her nerves, but Campbell was still walking in the clouds of post-wonderful Wynne Garrity sex, and she wasn't going to let anything bring her down. "Graham, although normally it would please me greatly for you to send me this missive, I know Ms. Garrity's number and will call her posthaste."

He beamed at her response, and she strolled back toward her office, pleased she'd made his day. Her euphoria lasted until she reached her door and saw Grace sitting in one of the chairs across from her desk. She made a show of looking over her shoulder. "Uh, if you like, maybe we can get you your own office."

"Don't be a smartass. Where have you been all morning?"

Campbell took a breath and searched for calm and a partial truth. "Working. Motion in the Leaderboard case. Judge's secretary said if we got it filed by noon, they could get us on Friday's docket. Why? Whatcha need?"

"I've got a lead on a pharmaceutical firm that's looking for new outside counsel. They'd prefer someone with a deeper bench, but I told them we could handle anything they throw our way. I know you have Rhea's depo to prep for, but I was hoping you could join me and Abby for a meeting at their office late this afternoon—a show of force like we did for Leaderboard."

"Absolutely." Motivated by guilt, Campbell blurted out her agreement before she could think of all the reasons it wasn't a good idea. She had planned to have dinner with Wynne and finalize her depo prep, but she owed this to Grace and Abby, and she wasn't going to let them down. "The depo isn't until tomorrow afternoon, so I'll have time for any last-minute prep in the morning."

"Perfect," Grace said. "I'll get you some notes before the meeting."

"Sounds great." Campbell sat at her desk and rummaged in her bag for her phone so she could call Wynne to let her know about the change in plans, but Grace wasn't showing any signs of leaving. Trying for nonchalance, she said, "Graham seems to be working out, although he has a very odd cadence to his speech. Kind of Renaissance fair meets *Downton Abbey*, but without the cool accent, if you know what I mean."

"Is there anything you'd like to tell me?"

Campbell's stomach sank. Grace knew about her and Wynne. Had Abby ratted her out? If she had, then she only knew part of the story, and not anything about what had happened last night. Still, if she was caught, she'd need to come clean about all of it. She couldn't have a big secret like this standing between her and her friends. "I can explain. I didn't mean for it to happen, but it did." She paused to think of a way to get Grace to see that what she felt for Wynne wouldn't interfere with her work, but Grace interrupted her.

"One day your impulsiveness is going to get you in big trouble, but now that it's here, Abby has fallen in love with it. I kind of like it too, but you have to stop buying things for the office without checking with us first. And we have to be able to afford it. Not just you, but all of us."

Campbell stared at Grace, while she tried to catch up, but after a minute, she gave up. "What are you talking about?"

"The circa nineteen sixty Coke bottle machine that's in the kitchen. Abby already has plans to stock it with beer and cider." Grace cocked her head. "What did you think I was talking about? Are there more deliveries on the way?"

Campbell forced a laugh to cover her relief. "No, I promise this is the last one." In the excitement over the Leaderboard case, she'd completely forgotten about the Coke machine that she'd found on eBay. "I'm glad you like it. I bought it a while back and had almost forgotten. I promise I got a great deal."

Grace stood. "You should go check it out. You know, before Abby fills it up with all her faves."

"I will. I just have one quick call to make and I'll be right there."

Campbell waited a few seconds after Grace shut the door, and then she let out a huge breath. *You should've told her.* She knew it was true, but she'd been so relieved to hear that Grace was calling her out about the Coke machine and not the fact she was sleeping with the enemy, that she'd clammed up. Plus it was pretty much impossible now to think of Wynne as the enemy. They'd been working well together, and she'd grown to like her. A lot. She'd seriously misjudged Wynne, thinking she was Stoltz's lackey, but after the way she took charge in the bedroom, Campbell knew she'd underestimated Wynne's independence, and Wynne in control was blazing hot.

Wynne answered her phone on the first ring. "Hey you."

"Hey yourself. Graham, our receptionist du jour, said that you called."

"I did. I have some bad news. Stoltz is coming back this afternoon instead of tomorrow, and he wants to meet tonight to get an update on how everything has gone so far, so I can't see you tonight."

Campbell was disappointed, but she could hear the regret in Wynne's voice and didn't want to pile on. "I totally get it. Besides we could both probably use a good night's sleep after last night, and I'm fairly certain that if we get together sleep is not on the agenda."

"I'll miss you tonight," Wynne said. "Is that weird to say?"

Campbell's heart fluttered as Wynne's words echoed her own feelings. "Don't ask me. I feel the same way."

"I'm sorry I'm not going to be able to help you get ready for Rhea's deposition."

"No worries. This way I can work without being distracted by your sexy self. How about I email you my outline later tonight? If you see anything that I need to add or change, we can work it out in the morning."

"Deal."

"And, Wynne?"

"Yes?"

"Text me when you're home for the night. Okay?" Her words were followed by a long pause. Either Wynne hadn't heard her, or she had and was offended. "Wynne?"

"I'm here."

"I hope that didn't sound presumptuous."

"It didn't. It was actually pretty sweet. Took me off guard."

"Because you don't think I'm sweet?"

"No, it's more like I'm not used to sweet."

Campbell heard the trace of sadness in Wynne's voice and wondered about the source. She made a mental note to ask her later. "Well, get used to it."

After they hung up, Campbell walked out of her office and headed toward the firm's combo kitchen/break room. She could hear Abby telling Grace what drinks she planned to load into the Coke machine, and the exuberance in Abby's voice made her smile. If she told them about Wynne right now, all that joy would be crushed under the weight of their worry about the impact of a Campbell-Wynne affair on their ability to win the competition for

Leaderboard's business. Little did they know that despite her sexy romp with Wynne, Campbell was ready to show Braxton Keith and everyone at Worth Ingram that she was capable of taking Rhea Hendricks and her frivolous lawsuit down, and she would start by knocking tomorrow's deposition out of the park.

Her revelation could wait one more day. Maybe two.

Wynne hung up from Campbell's call feeling melancholy. Campbell probably thought she was overly emotional, but she couldn't help it if she found Campbell's caretaking nature sweet and rare. People like her didn't come around every day.

She heard a knock on her door and looked up to see Jennifer framed in the doorway. "Come on in," Wynne said.

Jennifer handed her an envelope. "I just wanted to give you this and let you know that he's scheduled to land at six, and he'll be taking a car from the airport."

"Thanks. Any idea why he changed his plans?"

"Not a clue, but he called this morning and when you weren't here, he asked to speak to Daniel. I have no idea what they talked about."

Wynne didn't either. She shrugged it off. If Stoltz had an urgent need for something, he could've just called her on her cell. Considering more than half of his "urgent needs" involved mundane tasks that weren't even remotely time sensitive, she was secretly glad he'd reached Daniel instead of her.

Wynne reached for the interoffice envelope. "Do you know what's in here?"

Jennifer rolled her eyes. "I do, but you need to read it for yourself to get the full effect."

Wynne shook out the single sheet of paper. It was a memo from the firm's executive committee on what appeared to be new firm letterhead.

We are pleased to inform you that effective immediately, Worth, Ingram, Nash, and Reed will be utilizing a new firm logo and hereafter will be referred to by the acronym, WINR (pronounced "winner"), rather than Worth Ingram or any other permutation of the current full-length name. Our firm website has been updated, new stationary has been distributed to the staff, and you will be receiving new business cards shortly. It is our sincere hope that this new branding will appeal to a multigenerational audience and assist us in attracting diverse new business.

"They're kidding, right?" Jennifer shook her head, and Wynne pointed at her desk. "They want to attract a younger client base with more start-ups, so they're trying to be hip by using an acronym that sounds like a bad vanity plate. And what hip business sends out a printed memo in an ancient, interoffice envelope?"

"You're preaching to the choir," Jennifer said. "Time for you to make partner and change some things around here."

"Amen to that."

Wynne worked like a fiend the rest of the afternoon, stopping only once to forage in the break room fridge for one of the yogurts she kept at the office that other associates made fun of but loved to steal. She found a strawberry, not her favorite flavor, and started to peel back the lid when an image of Campbell, wearing only her robe and carrying a tray of breakfast tacos popped in her mind. Campbell wouldn't settle for a low-fat yogurt, and neither should she. She shoved the yogurt back in the fridge and pulled up a delivery app and ordered a pizza.

She stopped by Jennifer's desk on her way back to her office. Jen's brow was scrunched in a frown, but Wynne wrote it off to the chaos of Stoltz's schedule. "Hey, Jen, I just ordered a pizza, big enough for both of us in case you'd like to share. Can you let me know when it's here?"

"He's here," Jen whispered.

"What?" Wynne struggled to make sense of what she was saying. Her food couldn't be here already—no one made pizza that fast. "Who's here?" She watched Jen jerk her chin toward the closed door of Stoltz's office. Damn. "I thought he wasn't getting back until six at the earliest?"

"He took an earlier flight. He wants to see you."

Of course he did. Wynne's gut twisted, and her appetite disappeared. She hated when he went on these tears, and she hated even more not knowing what she was walking into. Based on previous experience, his client meetings hadn't gone well and he was looking for someone else to blame. She took a deep breath. "The pizza's already paid for. Just put it in the break room because I don't think I'll be having any. Do you mind tipping the pizza guy? I'll pay you back."

Jen waved her away. "I got it. And I'll save you a slice, just in case."

Wynne appreciated the gesture, but the idea of a greasy pizza on top of a Stoltz-induced ulcer was a complete no-go. Deciding to get this over with as quickly as possible, she marched up to Stoltz's door and knocked aggressively on the door.

"If that's you, Garrity, get in here."

She pushed through the door prepared to deal with whatever Stoltz planned to dish out. "What can I do for you?"

"For starters, you can start acting like a team player."

The veiled accusation was so out of left field, she wasn't sure how to respond. "I don't know what you're talking about. I'm fully committed to this team." She choked out the last word because Stoltz had never run their section like a team. He was the star, and they were all merely supporting players. She had dedicated every waking moment to making him shine, and she resented the implication she'd been anything but loyal. "I don't have any idea what you're talking about."

He handed her his phone. "Then would you like to explain these to me?"

She stared at the screen, confused about why he would have a photo of her on his phone. She looked up at him and he rolled his hand, motioning for her to keep looking, so she scrolled to the next photo and froze in place. She was wearing her sleeveless, cornflower blue shirt, and in the background was the bar at Winebelly, but those things were only context. The real focal point was her hands, laced through Campbell's hands, and her eyes gazing into hers. For a second, she was transported back to that moment—warm, inviting, full of portent. She'd had no idea she was being photographed. If she had, would she have changed anything about last night?

"Well?" Stoltz asked with a sneer.

"Where did you get this?"

"That's not important. What is important is that you seem to have a loyalty problem. We need Leaderboard's business, and it's up to you to make sure we keep it. Whatever is going on with you and this tramp, it needs to end now. She's using you so she can steal a client right out from under your nose. From now on, when you work together, you'll bring that clerk Donald, or David, whatever his name is along. He's your buffer so you don't let the pretty girl distract you from what's really important. Now, go. I want a thorough status report on my desk at eight thirty a.m., and I want you back in this chair ready to go over it with me. Get your head in the game, Garrity."

He picked up his phone and started punching numbers, his way of telling her she was dismissed. Her legs were wobbly when she stood, but she forced one foot in front of the other until she'd cleared his door. Jennifer shot her a sympathetic look as she walked past, but Wynne didn't pause to commiserate.

Wynne was angry, and she felt betrayed by whoever had taken that photo and given it to Stoltz, but she had to admit that in some respects, Stoltz was right. She never should've slept with Campbell while they were in competition. It muddied things between them, and although she didn't believe for one second that Campbell was using her, it had the appearance of impropriety even if neither one of them took advantage of their relationship to win Leaderboard's business.

But she had slept with Campbell, and she didn't regret it. Her one night with Campbell had been more fulfilling than all her dates with other women combined, and although she had no idea how they were going to make things work between them, she was committed to finding a way.

I should call her. Wynne pushed the thought away. Campbell was busy preparing for Rhea's deposition, and telling her about Stoltz's discovery would only be a distraction. Knowing Stoltz, he was probably banking on her telling Campbell about his suspicions to knock her off her game. Well, she wasn't going to do it. If she was going to win Leaderboard's future business, she was going to do so fair and square, and if everything went right, she would win Campbell too.

Chapter Nineteen

The next morning, Wynne poured her third cup of coffee and hoped it would do a better job at keeping her awake than the last two. After a rocky night of not much sleep, she'd come into the office at six a.m. and prepared an extensive status report on the case for Stoltz, complete with an index and the colored page separators that he liked. It contained copies of the complaint, answer, all the discovery, and an outline of their strategy for the case, "their" meaning the one she and Campbell had developed. She could've had Jennifer do the organizational part, but she wanted to convince Stoltz that she was fully committed even if it meant she basically worked around the clock.

She was almost finished when Jennifer buzzed through the intercom. "What's up?"

"He asked that you and Daniel meet him in the conference room."

"Okay, will you let Daniel know? I'll be right there." Wynne hung up and finished her prep, including the report for Stoltz in a three-ring binder. They were going to have to have a talk about his insistence that Daniel be her watchdog. She was a senior associate, and the idea of having a summer intern follow her around so he could report back to her boss was insulting and unacceptable. She'd discuss her feelings with Stoltz as soon as she wowed him with all the work she'd done so far as well as her plan for the rest of the case. She pushed through the doors of the conference room, prepared to do battle, but what she saw inside caught her completely off guard.

"Hi, Wynne, I hope I got the seating right." Brian, the court reporter, motioned to the table around which were seated Braxton Keith on one side, and Jeb Lawson, Rhea Hendricks's attorney, and Rhea Hendricks herself on the other. Daniel was sitting off to the side. A second later, Stoltz walked through the door completing the twilight zone experience of the entire tableau.

"Thanks, everyone for adjusting your schedule," Stoltz said. "Such flexibility is always appreciated. I just need a moment with Ms. Garrity, and then she'll be ready to get started." He motioned for her to follow and walked out of the room.

She waited until they were out of earshot of the conference room before confronting him. "What's going on?"

"Simple. One word: strategy."

His smile was smug, and she wanted to slap it off his face. "Rhea's deposition is scheduled for this afternoon. Campbell's doing it. It's been set for weeks."

"Schedules change. Everyone is here, and Campbell is nowhere in sight. Our client is paying by the hour, and I doubt he'd like to wait around for her to show up. This is your depo now. I trust you are prepared?"

Wynne opened her mouth to say no, but then she remembered the extremely thorough outline Campbell had sent her late last night. Despite the hour and the report she had to prepare for Stoltz, she'd carefully reviewed the outline, and offered a few suggestions, but not many, since it was practically perfect as it was. The outline was still on her computer, and it would only take a minute to print it out. Of course, in that same amount of time, she could place a call to Campbell and let her know what was going on.

"You have five seconds to make up your mind," Stoltz said. "Where does your loyalty belong? Remember your client is waiting."

Wynne looked down the hall, back toward the conference room door. She hadn't created this situation, and she'd never do something as underhanded as reschedule a deposition to thwart an opponent, but she had a duty to her client, and he was sitting in that room waiting for her to get started.

"Tell Daniel to go in my office, print the outline that's on my desktop, and bring it to me with a stack of Post-its, a yellow highlighter, and a red pen. There are discovery documents referenced in the outline, and he'll need to locate and bring me copies of those as well." She didn't wait for an answer before turning around and marching back to the conference room. Stoltz was likely apoplectic at being told what to do, but she'd deal with him later.

Braxton pulled her aside when she reentered the conference room. "Where's Campbell?"

"She was delayed," Wynne said, wishing that were the truth. "But I'm prepared and we're going to get started in just a minute." She smiled with a confidence she didn't feel. "Do you have any questions?"

"I can't think of anything right now."

"No problem." She pointed to one of the pads of paper on the table. "If you think of anything you want me to ask during the deposition, write it down and pass it to me. If I don't ask it in the moment, rest assured I have a plan. Either it's a timing issue and I plan to ask it later or there's a specific reason I don't want that information on the record. Pay close attention to how this goes because they'll be deposing you soon, and you can expect Lawson to be pretty rough on you. Take note of when Rhea's testimony is effective, and when it sounds like she's trying to hide something, and learn from what you see here today."

Braxton nodded obediently, and Wynne wondered when she'd become so damn bossy. First she was ordering Stoltz to fetch the intern, and then she was schooling her client. She was generally more deferential when it came to people in power, but Stoltz's stunt left her feeling rebellious.

Daniel walked in with a large file for her, and after a few minutes organizing the documents she planned to use as exhibits, she told Brian she was ready to get started. Like she had with the wedding planner, she started with a number of softball questions before she moved on to specific queries that focused on the causes of action Rhea had alleged in her lawsuit. Campbell's outline was intricate to the point of listing contingencies—if Rhea says X, then ask Y, but if she says A, then ask B—and Wynne followed it to the letter, eliciting line after line of testimony designed to support a motion to toss the case completely.

She was on a roll, and when Lawson requested a break, she was surprised to see they'd been going for almost three hours. Because it was close to noon, they agreed to go to lunch and resume at one thirty. Wynne hightailed it to her office, stopping at Jennifer's desk on the way. "Has Campbell called?"

"Yes, three times. I wasn't sure what to tell her, so I just said you were in a meeting. I hope that was okay."

Wynne sighed. The lie was less than ideal, but it wasn't Jennifer's fault Campbell was stuck in the middle of her feud with Stoltz. "Okay, I'm going to go call her."

"Oh, and Judge Pelman's office called. This week's trial is running over, but they've set the hearing on next Friday's docket at two p.m. Pelman's secretary wanted to know which one of you is going to handle the hearing."

"Tell them Wynne's going to handle it."

Wynne turned to see Braxton standing behind her. "I need to talk to Campbell first."

"No need," he said, shaking his head like it was a done deal. "You're on fire, and Campbell couldn't be bothered to show up. I know who I want to handle any court hearings, and that's you."

"What's going on?"

Wynne closed her eyes. She didn't need to look to know that Campbell had just arrived, on time for their planned last-minute prep for Rhea's deposition that should've been starting in an hour. She opened her eyes and turned to own her fate. "I can explain."

"Explain what? Did you start the deposition without me?"

Braxton stepped between them. "Campbell, I like you, but my board isn't going to sign off on counsel that lets the clock run while they are handling other people's business. Besides, Wynne is killing it in there. I'm going to stick to our arrangement and let your firm continue to work on the case, but I want Wynne to run point."

Campbell wore a puzzled expression, like Braxton's words hadn't registered, and Wynne was desperate to get her out of the lobby before she realized exactly what was going on. "Braxton, I need a minute with Campbell in my office. We'll see you after the break." She didn't wait for his answer before grabbing Campbell's arm and steering her away. She had a very short window to contain this fallout, and she prayed that Campbell would understand that she hadn't had a choice.

Campbell shook off Wynne's grasp as soon as they crossed the threshold to Wynne's office. She wanted answers and she wanted them now. "Do you mind telling me what's going on?"

"Have a seat?"

"I prefer to stand." Campbell crossed her arms. "Did you start Rhea's deposition without me? It's not scheduled to begin for another hour. Did you reschedule it without talking to me first? And when were you going to tell me? Last I heard from you was late last night when you emailed me to say I'd done a magnificent job on the prep. Did you know then?" She stopped even though she had more questions. Anger was fueling her reactions, but surely Wynne had an explanation for what was happening and why Brax suddenly thought she was irresponsible and incapable of acting as lead or even co-counsel.

"I can explain."

"You said that already. I'm waiting." Campbell watched a series of pained emotions cross Wynne's face. She was trying to give her the benefit of the doubt, but the longer she took to answer, the more Campbell's imagination spun out of control. Had she essentially just been fired from this case?

"Someone saw us at Winebelly." They took a picture and sent it to Stoltz. He rescheduled the deposition and insisted I handle it. I wanted to call you. I was about to call you just now when you showed up here."

"I showed up here because that was the plan," Campbell said, still trying to process everything Wynne had just said. "I'm not sure I'm following you. Stoltz has a picture of us?"

"Yes."

"Doing what, exactly?"

Wynne sighed. "Holding hands. Gazing into each other's eyes. You know, like girlfriends."

"Okay." Campbell shook her head. "I mean not okay. We agreed to play this fair and square, and let the best lawyer win. But Stoltz finds out we're…whatever, and suddenly you decide it's okay to cheat to get what you want?"

Wynne reached for her arm, but Campbell pulled away. She couldn't handle Wynne touching her right now because it might melt her anger, and she needed to stay angry because apparently when she let her guard down she got screwed. Wynne looked pained at the rebuff.

"I know that you're mad, and you have every right to be. I promise I'll straighten this out, but you have to see I didn't have a choice. Stoltz—"

"Stoltz is not your puppet master. You have the ability to make your own decisions. Tell me why you thought it was okay to do this to me, especially after…" Campbell couldn't say the words out loud because she was no longer certain what to call the night they'd spent together. In light of what had just happened, she definitely wouldn't call it lovemaking, but just calling it sex cheapened the deep longing she'd felt since.

Wynne's desk phone buzzed, and they both stared at it like it was an alien. It buzzed again, and Wynne picked it up. "Jennifer, I need a few more minutes."

Campbell wasn't trying to listen in, but she heard snippets of Jennifer's side of the conversation on the other end. "Emergency." "Only one call."

Wynne placed a hand over the phone. "I have to take this."

"Of course you do. I'm beginning to realize where I rate with you. Everything, especially anything work-related, is going to take precedence over anything personal in your life." Campbell strode toward the door. "Well, I'll make it easy for you. There is no more personal between me and you."

"Campbell, please."

Campbell was still facing the door. All she had to do was walk two more steps, turn the knob, and leave. Back to her own fledgling firm where she could explain to her partners that she'd managed to blow the first big case they had and lost their chance at any of Leaderboard's future business. How had she been so wrong? She never would've imagined Wynne would screw her over, even if ordered to do so by her asshole boss.

"Jennifer, please put the call through," Wynne said, apparently having moved on. "Dad, slow down. Are you okay? What happened. Are you hurt?"

Motivated by the fear in Wynne's voice, Campbell turned back around and walked toward Wynne's desk. Wynne was pale and shaking, clearly upset, and Campbell instinctively grabbed her free hand and squeezed it tight, watching and waiting to find out what had her on edge. Wynne scribbled some words on a piece of paper and assured her father she would take care of it. When she hung up, she slumped in her chair, still holding onto Campbell's hand.

"What's wrong?"

"My father's been arrested."

Campbell sat down on the edge of Wynne's desk and kept her voice calm and even. "Where is he?"

Wynne handed her the paper she'd been writing on. "Travis County jail."

Campbell looked at the paper, trying to decipher Wynne's notes, which were sparse. "Did he say what the charge was?"

"Gambling, but he didn't give details. He said they listen to the calls, and I don't even want to know how he knows that."

"Someone there probably told him that." Campbell looked at Wynne and tried to imagine how she must feel to get this kind of a call about one of her parents, which led her to realize she didn't know anything about Wynne's family. Was she an only child? Was that why her father had called her or was it because she was a lawyer? Where was Wynne's mother in this picture? "Is there someone you can call to help?"

"No. There's only my mother, and she's…she's not good at handling anything that involves being responsible." Wynne stood. "I have to go. I'll tell Stoltz. Maybe he can talk Lawson into letting you finish the deposition."

"Lawson will never agree to that. He probably won't agree to continue it either." Campbell stared at the paper on Wynne's desk. As betrayed as she felt, she hated seeing Wynne so shaken, torn between professional obligation and personal duty, but she understood. If Justin or Perry needed her, she'd drop everything to be there for them. She wished there was something she could do.

"I'll go." The words were out before she could stop them, but once they were, she was certain she was doing the right thing. There was no sense both of them losing Leaderboard's business over a botched sequence of events that had spiraled out of their control. "I'll go," she said again, more confidently this time. "I did an internship with Sturges and Lloyd my first summer in law school," she said, referring to a big shot criminal defense firm in town. "I may be a little rusty, but I think I can still find my way around the county jail."

"I can't ask you to do this."

"You're not." Campbell grabbed the paper from Wynne's desk. "I'll text you when I know something. Keep your phone with you in the deposition, just in case." She rushed out of the office before Wynne could stop her, but mostly before she could change her mind.

❖

The afternoon inched by. Using Campbell's meticulous outline, Wynne asked pointed questions and secured important admissions from Rhea Hendricks. Under normal circumstances, she would be excited about her success, but since her success came at the expense of Campbell's, she didn't deserve to celebrate.

Campbell had texted her an hour ago. *He's out on bond. More later.*

She could only hope there would be more later for her and Campbell. What kind of woman runs to the rescue within moments of finding out she'd been betrayed by the very woman she's rescuing?

The kind of woman you should hang on to.

Wynne knew her instincts were spot-on. She prayed Campbell would give her a chance to make things right, and she was committed to figuring out how as soon as she finished this deposition.

An hour later, she took a quick break to review Campbell's outline and decided she had all the information she needed to write a solid summary judgment motion to get this case kicked out of court. All thanks to Campbell.

Daniel followed her to her office. "Mr. Stoltz asked that we update him on how the deposition went as soon as it was over."

"Do you think I can have a minute to set my stuff down?" Wynne snapped, instantly regretful she was taking out her anger on the wrong person. "Sorry about that. It's been a long day. Tell *Mr.* Stoltz, I'll be there in a few minutes."

Daniel raised his hands and backed away, and she walked into her office, resenting Stoltz even more for assigning a watchdog to keep her in check. She started to shut her door so she could have a moment of peace before being called on the carpet, but Jennifer reached in and stopped her.

"She's back. I wasn't sure if you wanted to see her after everything that's happened today, but she insisted on waiting."

Wynne didn't have to ask who "she" was. "Please send her in." She lowered her voice. "And cover for me if someone comes looking, okay?"

"You got it."

Wynne waited by the door, and when Campbell walked in, she shut the door behind her. They were standing only a few feet apart, but the divide between them felt much larger. "I don't know how to thank you."

"I didn't do much. I got the name of a bonding company that would do a walk-thru so he could get out quicker than if he had to wait until the next magistrate hearing. He's been charged with keeping a gambling place. It's a Class A misdemeanor. He says he was working the door to a game room full of eight-liner machines for some extra cash. I talked to my contact at Sturges and Lloyd, Greg Paulson. He's the senior partner in their Austin office." Campbell handed her a card with Paulson's name and number. "You should give him a call. He's handled a bunch of these and said that if the owners of the game room will agree not to fight a forfeiture action for the machines and the cash that was seized, the DA's office will probably knock it down to a Class C misdemeanor, no more serious than a traffic ticket. Greg said the owners almost always agree to surrender the machines. They make so much money on them, they can afford to let some go."

Wynne breathed a huge sigh of relief. "Again, I don't know how to thank you." She stepped closer to Campbell, wanting to close both the physical and figurative distance between them. "And I'm so sorry for today. I chose security over doing the right thing. I know this doesn't change anything, but I've had to fight since I was a kid to have order in my life. Having parents who are essentially grifters makes me extra cautious about risking a sure thing. For the most part, that's worked to my benefit. I save money, I'm conservative with my investments, I've always managed to stay employed.

"Growing up, we were always having to move because Mom and Dad alienated someone who'd gotten involved in one of their get-rich quick schemes that never panned out. The house I live in? It was my grandmother's. She left it to them, and I bought it to keep them from mortgaging it away to fund their next big scheme." She paused, certain she was rambling, and unsure if Campbell even cared. As she fumbled for a way to make sense of her long story, Campbell reached for her hand.

"I hear you."

Wynne let out a breath, relieved that Campbell hadn't pushed her away, but then Campbell kept talking.

"But you had a choice to make and you chose your security, your job, over me. I'm not asking for special treatment because I'm attracted to you, or because we slept together, but I did expect that you would treat me with respect. Today was my chance to shine, but you were in the spotlight. And you are brilliant and smart and you deserve to be in the spotlight. But not at my expense."

Wynne nodded. Everything Campbell said was true. "Can I make it up to you?"

"I don't see how."

Campbell looked down at their still joined hands and eased her fingers loose. Wynne watched their connection break and felt her heart breaking as well.

Chapter Twenty

Campbell set her tray down and slid into the seat across from Justin. "Thanks for meeting me all the way out here."

"You said the two magic phrases. Mighty Fine Burgers and you're buying. I gotta say though, you're kind of overdressed for a burger joint."

Campbell looked down at her suit. It was her favorite, the one she'd worn for the Leaderboard pitch, and the white jacket probably wasn't the best choice to wear when chowing down on a juicy burger. But it had brought her luck before, and she was counting on it still having some magic left. It had been almost a week since she'd walked away from Wynne and the Leaderboard case. Well, technically she was still on the Leaderboard case, but relegated to spectator status, since Wynne and Worth Ingram were now officially lead counsel. Thankfully, there had been no reason for her to have to interact with anyone from Worth Ingram since she'd last seen Wynne.

She'd come clean to Grace and Abby about everything. How she'd let her relationship with Wynne become personal, how she'd gotten tricked out of taking the lead on Rhea's deposition and consequently, the whole case. After a big lecture from Grace, and some gentle advice from Abby about impulsivity and not letting sex cloud her judgment, they'd both said they forgave her, but she still felt like she needed to get back out there and find a big, new client if for no other reason than to avoid their disappointed looks around the office. Hence the suit. "I'm headed to a networking function this afternoon. I need some new clients. I blew it with Leaderboard. Over a girl."

Justin chased a big bite of burger with a swig from his Coke bottle. "If I had to count the number of times I messed up because of a girl, well, let's just say I'm glad I don't have to. Was she worth it?"

"Yes. No. I mean, I thought so at the time, but it turns out I was wrong. We were competing and she beat me, but she cheated. Actually, her boss cheated, and she went along." She stopped talking as she realized that unless she told him every detail, nothing she was saying would make any sense. And she had no desire to rehash the entire episode. "The bottom line is it's over."

"Sure it is."

She grew defensive at his sarcastic tone. "It is."

"Yep, it sounds like you're completely over her."

"I didn't say I was over her. I said it was over."

"Quit speaking lawyer to me. I get the difference, but if you're not over her, then it's not really over. Trust me. I'm older and wiser."

"Said the bachelor."

He reached over and stole a fry. "I don't have to be married to know about relationships. It's a matter of pros and cons. Do you like her more than you don't? Is this thing that came between you enough to tip the balance in the other direction? Is it unforgivable? You and I both know that life's too short to let temporary hurt feelings get in the way of long-term happiness."

She resisted pointing out that getting marginalized on a big case and losing any chance at future business from the client she'd worked so hard to win was more than a temporary hurt feeling, but she knew there was some truth in his words. Wynne had been caught in a hard spot, and she'd made a snap decision. Campbell didn't think she'd do the same, but what if it had been Grace or

Abby who'd asked her to choose between the business and her feelings for Wynne? "I don't know what to do."

"Then don't do anything." He laughed when she stuck out her tongue. "I get how hard it is for you to just let things be, but you could do with a little chill time. You can't always make things work. Sometimes you have to let life happen."

"When did you get to be so wise?"

"I've always been wise. You're just getting smart enough to notice," he said with a grin, while holding up his arm to block her punch.

A half hour later, Campbell reflected on his words on the way to her function. She'd taken a big leap of faith by quitting her job and hadn't once regretted her decision despite the uncertainty. Yes, she had a generous nest egg, but she also had two friends whose futures relied on their firm's success. But when it came to her heart, she preferred rock solid certainty that she was entrusting her feelings to someone she could count on. A week ago, she would've trusted Wynne to be that person. She'd even started to think that Wynne might be the one. Had one action completely decimated that trust or was she asking too much?

Justin's advice might be solid after all. She should just let it be. Whatever she'd had with Wynne was over. Mourn the loss and move on. That last part was easier said than done.

Wynne saw Seth out of the corner of her eye and motioned for him to hang on while she finished typing the last sentence of her notes. When she looked up from her computer, he leaned back in one of the chairs across from her desk and put his feet up. "To what do I owe this visit?"

"Just seeing if you are alive. You've been ignoring my texts."

"I have not."

"Replying with single emoticons is essentially the same as ignoring me," he said.

"Has anyone ever told you that you are attention starved?"

"Yes. You have told me this many times. Want to know the best cure for my condition?"

"Not really."

"More attention," he said, smacking the arm of the chair for emphasis.

"Seth, I'm busy."

"We've had this conversation. You're always busy, but lately you're busy and sad. I have a solution and it's called happy hour. Meet me after work? Patent section is buying again."

At the mention of the patent section, Wynne felt her jaw clench. "No thanks."

Seth narrowed his eyes. "What just happened?"

"Nothing. I'm not interested."

"Come on, Wynne. I can tell when you're mad. Have I done something to upset you?"

She looked into his eyes and saw genuine concern. "It's not you. I found out that your pal Lane was the one who sent the pictures of me and Campbell to Stoltz. What kind of bitch do you have to be to do something like that?"

"Holy shit, for real?"

"Jennifer saw the email and overheard Lane gossiping about it with one of the other patent attorneys. Apparently, Lane had just met with a client at Winebelly and came back because she'd left her credit card. She saw us and decided Stoltz needed photographic evidence of my indiscretion. But if you repeat that, I will never ever go to happy hour with you again. Needless to say, I have no desire to run into Lane again."

"Nor do I. Not even to let her and her brainiac friends buy me drinks. Hashtag solidarity."

"You need to quit saying the word hashtag. It's kind of nerdy."

"So, hashtag nerds unite would not be appropriate in this situation?"

She tossed a paperclip at him. "Seriously. Stop."

"Okay, but this is even more reason why you need a happy hour in your future."

"I don't want to drink. I want…" She didn't finish her sentence because what was the point? Campbell had walked out, making it crystal clear that there was no future for them outside of this case, and judging by the fact Campbell hadn't contacted her about the case either, she wasn't sure they had any relationship at all.

"You want Campbell," Seth said, his words echoing her loss.

"Yes, but I can't have her."

"Can't is for quitters."

"She walked away."

"And you let her. Seriously, it's like I have to spell everything out for you. You screwed her over, and she still stepped up for you with your dad, who I would have left to rot in jail, by the way." She started to interrupt, but he held up a hand to stop her. "That's a subject for another day. Back to Campbell. The ball's in your court now. How did you leave things?"

"Badly." At his frown, she searched her memory, but she didn't have to look hard, as their final words to each other were burned in her brain. "I asked her how I could make it up to her and she said she didn't see how."

"Bingo." Seth slapped the arm of the chair again. "She doesn't see how because it's up to you. This is a grand gesture moment if I've ever seen one." He waved his arms in the air. "You have to do something big to win her back."

"Like what?"

"Nuh-uh, this is where my assistance ends." He pointed to his chest. "Whatever you do has to come from your heart."

"Lovely. We both know how good I am with feelings."

"Don't try so hard. Relax and the right thing will come to you." He stood. "Once you come up with your grand idea, let me know if you need help with the execution. In the meantime, my work here is done."

The room felt very empty when he left, and Wynne's mind buzzed with plenty of recrimination, but no tangible solutions to win Campbell back. Seth's words echoed, and she closed her eyes and leaned back in her chair to relax. It took a while, but finally her brain stopped spinning and she experienced a gentle wave of calm followed by a moment of intense clarity that revealed the grand idea she knew would give her the best chance at a second chance with Campbell. The only question was whether she had the courage to take the leap.

CHAPTER TWENTY-ONE

Campbell walked into the lobby and nodded to Graham who was on the phone. He hung up as she passed his desk and said, "Good morning, Ms. Clark."

"Good morning, Graham. And you can call me Campbell."

"Will do, Ms. Clark."

Campbell smiled. He was beginning to grow on her, and she should really stop fighting his strong desire to be formal. She should stop other things too, like succumbing to this persistent sadness that followed her around like a black cloud. It had only been a day since she'd been trying to follow Justin's advice to just let things be, but she still couldn't shake the desire to do something about her lingering feelings for Wynne, and her mood was affecting her relationship with Grace and Abby as well.

That was something she could fix. "Graham, please alert Ms. Keane and Ms. Maldonado, and request their presence in the conference room. Posthaste."

"Absolutely. Your wish is my command."

Campbell saluted him, because it seemed like the thing to do, and strode to the conference room to wait for her partners.

"What's up?" Grace said as she walked into the room with Abby close behind. "Did you buy another cool appliance for the office or maybe a company car?"

"I'm hoping she brought baked goods," Abby said, looking around at the empty table. "Seriously, no pastries?"

Campbell raised her hands. "You're both very funny. I come bearing no gifts, food or otherwise." She motioned for them to have a seat. "I want to apologize."

Abby waved her off. "Done and done. We've forgiven you."

"Yes, you have, for the whole Leaderboard thing, but I know it's bigger than that. I have a tendency to make decisions based on emotion without considering the big picture. Not just the Leaderboard thing, but this conference table, and the Coke machine, and well, you get the idea. I just wanted to let you know that I'm going to work on being less impulsive and focus on making decisions based on what makes sense for all of us, not just my personal gut feelings." She folded her hands on the table and watched for their reactions. Both of them looked like they were about to burst, but neither said anything. "Well?"

Like a flip had been switched, they both started laughing uncontrollably with no sign of stopping.

"What's going on?" Campbell asked, unsure if they could hear her through their gales of laughter.

Abby held up a hand until her chuckling was under control. "You can't change."

"I can too. And I'm going to. I promise."

"No," Abby said, shaking her head. "We don't want you to. If you weren't impulsive we'd all still be working for assholes like Jerry Stoltz. It may take us a while to make a go of this, but at least we're in charge. Right, Grace?"

"Right. Campbell, you frustrate the hell out of me sometimes, but I wouldn't change your Big Idea brain for anything. Besides, Abby and I have become very attached to our new drink dispenser."

"And don't forget the espresso maker," Abby said.

"I wonder what's next?" Grace asked, sending the three of them into a giggling fit.

They were still giggling when Graham entered the room. "Ladies, you have guests."

Campbell struggled to contain herself, but she just couldn't. "Pray tell, announce them to us."

Graham nodded and waved his arm in a flourish. "I shall fetch Mr. Keith and Ms. Garrity."

Instantly, the room sobered. "What are they doing here?" Campbell asked, but Graham was already gone, presumably to "fetch" Brax and Wynne.

Abby stood. "You stay here. We got this. Grace, are you with me?"

"On it."

"No, wait." Campbell stood too. "Let me." The uncontrollable bout of laughter had left her feeling free. She'd cleared the air with Abby and Grace. Now it was time to do the same with Wynne. "I need to see her."

With her friends on her heels, Campbell strode into the lobby. Wynne was pacing in front of Graham's desk, and Brax was asking her what they were doing here. Wynne started to answer him, but stopped and locked eyes with Campbell. For a few seconds, the world stopped and it was just the two of them, standing a few feet apart, as they had been the last time Campbell had seen her, but the hurt had fallen away and Campbell could only see the passionate, beautiful woman she'd made love to.

"I still don't know why we're here," Brax said before following Wynne's gaze. "Hi, Campbell. Are we here to meet with you about the case?"

"Yes," Wynne said before Campbell could answer. "But not really about the case. More like about your future, Brax. Can I get you all to step outside for a minute?"

She started walking toward the door without waiting for a response. Abby and Grace looked at Campbell who nodded, and the three of them followed Wynne and Brax out to the parking lot where Kate's donut truck was pulling into the parking lot. As if on cue, the truck came to a stop, and Kate opened the window and waved at her brother and then at Campbell who smiled and waved back. She had no idea what was happening, but if it involved donuts, it had to be good.

Wynne stepped in front of the truck. "Brax, I asked Kate to bring her truck here for two reasons. First, I did some research, and found out that you have Kate's truck on your corporate campus because having your sister there serving her homemade donuts makes it feel like home. I thought it only appropriate then, that Kate be here for this announcement. Clark, Keane, and Maldonado should be your new home base for all your legal needs. I'm smart and I've always worked hard for you, but Campbell Clark is the whole package. She's got a brilliant mind, charisma, and she's quick on her feet.

"I handled Rhea's deposition last week using Campbell's meticulous outline, and the motions we've filed were all written by her. You thought Campbell wasn't there for you, and I let you believe that because I had a boss that insisted I do whatever it takes to win, even if that meant screwing over a colleague. I no longer work for Worth Ingram, so if you elect to go with them, Jerry Stoltz will be handling all your work. Just let that sink in for a minute, and I think you know the choice is clear.

"Now, if you all don't mind, I'd like to get a word alone with Campbell, but if you all want to step up to the window, the donuts are on me."

Campbell stood frozen in place as she digested Wynne's words. Had she really quit her job?

"Are you okay?" Abby whispered in her ear.

"I think so."

"You better work it out real quick because she's on her way over here, and she doesn't look like she's going to take no for an answer."

Campbell nodded, her eyes trained on Wynne as she approached and the rest of the world fell away. "Donuts. Smooth move. What was your second reason for having Kate here?"

"To win you over, of course," Wynne said. "Some might say I'm trying to exploit your weakness."

Campbell grinned. "I'm learning that I have a lot of weakness when it comes to you."

"I'm truly sorry for taking advantage."

"You were protecting yourself. I get it. I really do." Campbell couldn't stand to see the pained look on Wynne's face, so she changed the subject. "Did you really quit your job?"

"Best thing I ever did. I'm going to take some time and figure out what to do, but I'm never going to work for an asshole again. Just one more thing I learned from you."

"Oh, really, what else have you learned?"

"To pay attention to my feelings, to go after what I want, even if it means taking a risk." Wynne stepped closer, her eyes dark and her gaze intense. "I want you, Campbell Clark. You're the best thing that's ever happened to me, and I hope I'm not too late to tell you I'm falling in love with you. Will you give us another chance?"

Campbell's sixth sense told her that Abby, Grace, Kate, and Brax, probably even Graham were all watching, donuts in hand, waiting to hear what she would say, but in that moment, no one else mattered but the beautiful, vulnerable woman standing directly in front of her, and she didn't care if the world heard her answer. "Yes, absolutely yes."

About the Author

Carsen Taite is a recovering lawyer who prefers writing fiction to practicing law because she has more control of the outcome. She believes that lawyers make great lovers, which is why she includes so many of them in her novels. She is the award-winning author of over twenty novels of romance and romantic intrigue, including the Luca Bennett Bounty Hunter series, the Lone Star Law series, and the Legal Affairs romances.

Books Available from Bold Strokes Books

Accidental Prophet by Bud Gundy. Days after his grandmother dies, Drew Morten learns his true identity and finds himself racing against time to save civilization from the apocalypse. (978-1-63555-452-6)

Create a Life to Love by Erin Zak. When sixteen-year-old Beth shows up at her birth mother's door, three lives will change forever. (978-1-63555-425-0)

Daughter of No One by Sam Ledel. When their worlds are threatened, a princess and a village outcast must overcome their differences and embrace a budding attraction if they want to survive. (978-1-63555-427-4)

Fear of Falling by Georgia Beers. Singer Sophie James is ready to shake up her career, but her new manager, the gorgeous Dana Landon, has other ideas. (978-1-63555-443-4)

In Case You Forgot by Fredrick Smith and Chaz Lamar. Zaire and Kenny, two newly single, Black, queer, and socially aware men, start again—in love, career, and life—in the West Hollywood neighborhood of LA. (978-1-63555-493-9)

Playing with Fire by Lesley Davis. When Takira Lathan and Dante Groves meet at Takira's restaurant, love may find its way onto the menu. (978-1-63555-433-5)

Practice Makes Perfect by Carsen Taite. Meet law school friends Campbell, Abby, and Grace, law partners at Austin's premier boutique legal firm for young, hip entrepreneurs. Legal Affairs: one law firm, three best friends, three chances to fall in love. (978-1-63555-357-4)

The Last Seduction by Ronica Black. When you allow true love to elude you once and you desperately regret it, are you brave enough to grab it when it comes around again? (978-1-63555-211-9)

Wavering Convictions by Erin Dutton. After a traumatic event, Maggie has vowed to regain her strength and independence. So how can Ally be both the woman who makes her feel safe and a constant reminder of the person who took her security away? (978-1-63555-403-8)

A Bird of Sorrow by Shea Godfrey. As Darrius and her lover, Princess Jessa, gather their strength for the coming war, a mysterious spell will reveal the truth of an ancient love. (978-1-63555-009-2)

All the Worlds Between Us by Morgan Lee Miller. High school senior Quinn Hughes discovers that a broken friendship is actually a door propped open for an unexpected romance. (978-1-63555-457-1)

An Intimate Deception by CJ Birch. Flynn County Sheriff Elle Ashley has spent her adult life atoning for her wild youth, but when she finds her ex, Jessie, murdered two weeks before the small town's biggest social event, she comes face-to-face with her past and all her well-kept secrets. (978-1-63555-417-5)

Cash and the Sorority Girl by Ashley Bartlett. Cash Braddock doesn't want to deal with morality, drugs, or people. Unfortunately, she's going to have to. (978-1-63555-310-9)

Counting for Thunder by Phillip Irwin Cooper. A struggling actor returns to the Deep South to manage a family crisis, finds love, and ultimately his own voice as his mother is regaining hers for possibly the last time. (978-1-63555-450-2)

Falling by Kris Bryant. Falling in love isn't part of the plan, but will Shaylie Beck put her heart first and stick around, or tell the damaging truth? (978-1-63555-373-4)

Secrets in a Small Town by Nicole Stiling. Deputy Chief Mackenzie Blake has one mission: find the person harassing Savannah Castillo and her daughter before they cause real harm. (978-1-63555-436-6)

Stormy Seas by Ali Vali. The high-octane follow-up to the best-selling action-romance, *Blue Skies*. (978-1-63555-299-7)

The Road to Madison by Elle Spencer. Can two women who fell in love as girls overcome the hurt caused by the father who tore them apart? (978-1-63555-421-2)

Dangerous Curves by Larkin Rose. When love waits at the finish line, dangerous curves are a risk worth taking. (978-1-63555-353-6)

Love to the Rescue by Radclyffe. Can two people who share a past really be strangers? (978-1-62639-973-0)

Love's Portrait by Anna Larner. When museum curator Molly Goode and benefactor Georgina Wright uncover a portrait's secret, public and private truths are exposed, and their deepening love hangs in the balance. (978-1-63555-057-3)

Model Behavior by MJ Williamz. Can one woman's instability shatter a new couple's dreams of happiness? (978-1-63555-379-6)

Pretending in Paradise by M. Ullrich. When travelwisdom.com assigns PR specialist Caroline Beckett and travel blogger Emma Morgan to cover a hot new couples retreat, they're forced to fake a relationship to secure a reservation. (978-1-63555-399-4)

Recipe for Love by Aurora Rey. Hannah Little doesn't have much use for fancy chefs or fancy restaurants, but when New York City chef Drew Davis comes to town, their attraction just might be a recipe for love. (978-1-63555-367-3)

Survivor's Guilt and Other Stories by Greg Herren. Award-winning author Greg Herren's short stories are finally pulled together into a single collection, including the Macavity Award nominated title story and the first-ever Chanse MacLeod short story. (978-1-63555-413-7)

The House by Eden Darry. After a vicious assault, Sadie, Fin, and their family retreat to a house they think is the perfect place to start over, until they realize not all is as it seems. (978-1-63555-395-6)

Uninvited by Jane C. Esther. When Aerin McLeary's body becomes host for an alien intent on invading Earth, she must work with researcher Olivia Ando to uncover the truth and save humankind. (978-1-63555-282-9)

Comrade Cowgirl by Yolanda Wallace. When cattle rancher Laramie Bowman accepts a lucrative job offer far from home, will her heart end up getting lost in translation? (978-1-63555-375-8)

Double Vision by Ellie Hart. When her cell phone rings, Giselle Cutler answers it—and finds herself speaking to a dead woman. (978-1-63555-385-7)

Inheritors of Chaos by Barbara Ann Wright. As factions splinter and reunite, will anyone survive the final showdown between gods and mortals on an alien world? (978-1-63555-294-2)

Love on Lavender Lane by Karis Walsh. Accompanied by the buzz of honeybees and the scent of lavender, Paige and Kassidy must find a way to compromise on their approach to business if they want to save Lavender Lane Farm—and find a way to make room for love along the way. (978-1-63555-286-7)

Spinning Tales by Brey Willows. When the fairy tale begins to unravel and villains are on the loose, will Maggie and Kody be able to spin a new tale? (978-1-63555-314-7)

The Do-Over by Georgia Beers. Bella Hunt has made a good life for herself and put the past behind her. But when the bane of her high school existence shows up for Bella's class on conflict resolution, the last thing they expect is to fall in love. (978-1-63555-393-2)

What Happens When by Samantha Boyette. For Molly Kennan, senior year is already an epic disaster, and falling for mysterious waitress Zia is about to make life a whole lot worse. (978-1-63555-408-3)

Wooing the Farmer by Jenny Frame. When fiercely independent modern socialite Penelope Huntingdon-Stewart and traditional country farmer Sam McQuade meet, trusting their hearts is harder than it looks. (978-1-63555-381-9)

A Chapter on Love by Laney Webber. When Jannika and Lee reunite, their instant connection feels like a gift, but neither is ready for a second chance at love. Will they finally get on the same page when it comes to love? (978-1-63555-366-6)

Drawing Down the Mist by Sheri Lewis Wohl. Everyone thinks Grand Duchess Maria Romanova died in 1918. They were almost right. (978-1-63555-341-3)

Listen by Kris Bryant. Lily Croft is inexplicably drawn to Hope D'Marco but will she have the courage to confront the consequences of her past and present colliding? (978-1-63555-318-5)

Perfect Partners by Maggie Cummings. Elite police dog trainer Sara Wright has no intention of falling in love with a coworker, until Isabel Marquez arrives at Homeland Security's Northeast Regional Training facility and Sara's good intentions start to falter. (978-1-63555-363-5)

Shut Up and Kiss Me by Julie Cannon. What better way to spend two weeks of hell in paradise than in the company of a hot, sexy woman? (978-1-63555-343-7)

Spencer's Cove by Missouri Vaun. When Foster Owen and Abigail Spencer meet they uncover a story of lives adrift, loves lost, and true love found. (978-1-63555-171-6)

Without Pretense by TJ Thomas. After living for decades hiding from the truth, can Ava learn to trust Bianca with her secrets and her heart? (978-1-63555-173-0)

Unexpected Lightning by Cass Sellars. Lightning strikes once more when Sydney and Parker fight a dangerous stranger who threatens the peace they both desperately want. (978-1-163555-276-8)